beethoven was one-sixteenth black

and other stories

Nadine Gordimer

beethoven
was
one-sixteenth
black
and other
stories

BLOOMSBURY

First published in Great Britain 2007
This collection Copyright © 2007 by Nadine Gordimer

Individual stories:
Copyright © 2004, 2005, 2006, 2007 by Nadine Gordimer
Copyright © 2002, 2004 by Felix Licensing BV

The moral right of the author has been asserted

Bloomsbury Publishing Plc
36 Soho Square
London WID 3QY

www.bloomsbury.com
Bloomsbury Publishing, London, New York and Berlin
A CIP catalogue record for this book is available from the British Library

ISBN 9780747592334
10 9 8 7 6 5 4 3 2 1

Printed in Great Britain by Clays Limited, St Ives plc

The paper this book is printed on is certified by the
© 1996 Forest Stewardship Council A.C. (FSC).
It is ancient-forest friendly.
The printer holds FSC chain of custody SCS-COC-2061

FSC
Mixed Sources
Product group from well-managed
forests and other controlled sources
Cert no. SGS-COC-2061
www.fsc.org
© 1996 Forest Stewardship Council

REINHOLD

2007

contents

beethoven was
one-sixteenth black

Beethoven was one-sixteenth black

　　　the presenter of a classical music programme on the
radio announces along with the names of musicians who will
be heard playing the String Quartets no. 13, op. 130, and
no. 16, op. 135.

Does the presenter make the claim as restitution for
Beethoven? Presenter's voice and cadence give him away as
irremediably white. Is one-sixteenth an unspoken wish for
himself.

Once there were blacks wanting to be white.

Now there are whites wanting to be black.

It's the same secret.

Frederick Morris (of course that's not his name, you'll soon
catch on I'm writing about myself, a man with the same ini-
tials) is an academic who teaches biology and was an activist

3

back in the apartheid time, among other illegal shenanigans an amateur cartoonist of some talent who made posters depicting the regime's leaders as the ghoulish murderers they were and, more boldly, joined groups to paste these on city walls. At the university, new millennium times, he's not one of the academics the student body (a high enrolment robustly black, he approves) singles out as among those particularly reprehensible, in protests against academe as the old white male crowd who inhibit transformation of the university from a white intellectuals' country club to a non-racial institution with a black majority (politically-correct-speak). Neither do the students value much the support of whites, like himself, dissident from what's seen as the other, the gowned body. You can't be on somebody else's side. That's the reasoning? History's never over; any more than biology, functioning within every being.

One-sixteenth. The trickle seemed enough to be asserted out of context? What does the distant thread of blood matter in the genesis of a genius. Then there's Pushkin, if you like; his claim is substantial, look at his genuine frizz on the head—not some fashionable faked Afro haloing a white man or woman, but coming, it's said, from Ethiopia.

Perhaps because he's getting older—Morris doesn't know he's still young enough to think fifty-two is old—he reflects occasionally on what was lived in his lifeline-before-him. He's divorced, a second time; that's a past, as well, if rather immediate. His father was also not a particular success as a family man. Family: the great-grandfather, dead long before the boy was born: there's a handsome man, someone from an old oval-framed photograph, the strong looks not passed on. There are stories about this forefather, probably related at family gatherings but hardly listened to by a boy impatient to leave the grown-ups' table. Anecdotes not in the history book obliged to be learned by rote. What might call upon amused recognition to be adventures, circumstances taken head-on, good times enjoyed out of what others would submit to as bad times, characters—'they don't make them like that any more'—as enemies up to no good, or joined forces with as real mates. No history-book events: tales of going about your own affairs within history's fall-out. He was some sort of frontiersman, not in the colonial military but in the fortune-hunters' motley.

A descendant in the male line, Frederick Morris bears his surname, of course. Walter Benjamin Morris apparently was always called Ben, perhaps because he was the Benjamin indeed of the brood of brothers who did not, like him, emigrate to Africa. No-one seems to know why he did; just an adventurer, or maybe the ambition to be rich which didn't appear to be achievable anywhere other than a beckoning Elsewhere. He might have chosen the Yukon. At home in London he was in line to inherit the Hampstead delicatessen shop, see it full of cold cuts and pickles, he was managing for another one of the fathers in the family line, name lost. He was married for only a year when he left. Must have convinced his young bride that their future lay in his going off to prospect for the newly discovered diamonds in a far place called Kimberley, from where he would promptly return rich. As a kind of farewell surety for their love, he left inside her their son to be born.

Frederick surprises his mother by asking if she kept the old attaché case—a battered black bag, actually—where once his father had told him there was stuff about the family they should go through some time; both had forgotten this rendezvous, his father had died before that time came. He did not have much expectation that she still kept the case somewhere, she had moved from what had been the home of marriage and disposed of possessions for which there was no room, no place in her life in a garden complex of elegant contemporary-design cottages. There were some things in a communal storeroom tenants had use of. There he found the bag and squatting among the detritus of other people's pasts he blew away the silverfish moths from letters and scrap jottings, copied the facts recorded above. There are also photographs, mounted on board, too tough for whatever serves silverfish as jaws, which he took with him, didn't think his mother would be sufficiently interested in for him to inform her. There is one portrait in an elaborate frame.

The great-grandfather has the same stance in all the photographs whether he is alone beside a photographer's studio palm or among piles of magical dirt, the sieves that would sift from the earth the rough stones that were diamonds within their primitive forms, the expressionless blacks and half-coloured men leaning on spades. Prospectors from London and Paris and Berlin—anywhere where there are no diamonds— did not themselves race to stake their claims when the starter's gun went off, the hired men who belonged on the land they ran over were swifter than any white foreigner, they staked the foreigners' claims and wielded the picks and spades in the open-cast mining concessions these marked. Even when Ben Morris is photographed sitting in a makeshift overcrowded bar his body, neck tendons, head are upright as if he were standing so immovably confident—of what? (Jottings reveal that he unearthed only small stuff. Negligible carats.) Of virility. That's unmistakable, it's untouched by the fickleness of fortune. Others in the picture have become slumped and shabbied by poor luck. The aura of sexual virility in the composure, the dark, bright, on-the-lookout inviting eyes: a call to the other sex as well as elusive diamonds. Women must have heard, read him the way males didn't, weren't meant to. Dates on the scraps of paper made delicately lacy by insects show that he didn't return promptly, he prospected with obstinate faith in his quest, in himself, for five years.

He didn't go home to London, the young wife, he saw the son only once on a single visit when he impregnated the young wife and left her again. He did not make his fortune; but he must have gained some slowly accumulated profit from the small stones the black men dug for him from their earth, because after five years it appears he went back to London and used his acquired knowledge of the rough stones to establish himself in the gem business, with connections in Amsterdam.

The great-grandfather never returned to Africa. Frederick's mother can at least confirm this, since her son is interested. The later members of the old man's family—his fertility produced more sons, from one of whom Frederick is descended—came for other reasons, as doctors and lawyers, businessmen, conmen and entertainers, to a level of society created from profit of the hired fast-runners' unearthing of diamonds and gold for those who had come from beyond the seas, another kind of elsewhere.

And that's another story. You're not responsible for your ancestry, are you.

But if that's so, why have marched under banned slogans, got yourself beaten up by the police, arrested a couple of times; plastered walls with subversive posters. That's also the past. The past is valid only in relation to whether the present recognises it.

How did that handsome man with the beckoning gaze, the characteristic slight flare of the nostrils as if picking up some tempting scent (in every photograph), the strong beringed hands (never touched a spade) splayed on tight-trousered thighs, live without his pretty London bedmate all the nights of prospecting? And the Sunday mornings when you wake, alone, and don't have to get up and get out to educate the students in the biological facts of life behind their condomed cavortings—even a diamond prospector must have lain a while longer in his camp bed, Sundays, known those surges of desire, and no woman to turn to. Five years. Impossible that a healthy male, as so evidently this one, went five years without making love except for the brief call on the conjugal bed. Never mind the physical implication; how sad. But of course it wasn't so. He obviously didn't have to write and confess to his young wife that he was having an affair—this is the past, not the sophisticated protocol of suburban sexual freedom—it's unimaginably makeshift, rough as the diamonds. There were those black girls who came to pick up prospectors' clothes for washing (two in the background of a photograph where, barechested, the man has fists up, bunched in a mock fight with a swinging-bellied mate at the diggings) and the half-black girls (two coffee one milk the description at the time) in confusion of a bar-tent caught smiling, passing him carrying high their trays of glasses. Did he have many of these girls over those years of deprived nights and days. Or was there maybe a special one, several special ones, there are no crude circumstances, Frederick himself has known, when there's not a possibility of tenderness coming uninvited to the straightforward need for a fuck. And the girls. What happened to the girls if in male urgencies there was conception. The foreigners come to find diamonds came and went, their real lives with women were Elsewhere, intact far away. What happened? Are there children's children of those conceptions on-the-side engendered by a handsome prospector who went home to his wife and sons and the gem business in London and Amsterdam—couldn't they be living where he propagated their predecessors.

Frederick knows as everyone in a country of many races does that from such incidents far back there survives proof in the appropriation, here and there, of the name that was all the progenitor left behind him, adopted without his knowledge or consent out of—sentiment, resentment, something owed? More historical fall-out. It was not in mind for a while, like the rendezvous with the stuff in the black bag, forgotten with his father. There was a period of renewed disturbances at the university, destruction of equipment within the buildings behind their neo-classical columns; not in the Department of Biology, fortunately.

The portrait of his great-grandfather in its oval frame under convex glass that had survived unbroken for so long stayed propped up where the desk moved to his new apartment was placed when he and his ex-wife divided possessions. Photographs give out less meaning than painted portraits. Open less contemplation. But *he* is there, he is—a statement.

One-sixteenth black.

In the telephone directory for what is now a city where the diamonds were first dug, are there any listings of the name Morris. Of course there will be, it's not uncommon and so has no relevance.

As if he has requested her to reserve cinema tickets with his credit card he asks his secretary to see if she can get hold of a telephone directory for a particular region. There are Morrises and Morrisons. In his apartment he calls up the name on the internet one late night, alone. There's a Morris who is a theatre director now living in Los Angeles and a Morris a champion bridge player in Cape Town. No-one of that name in Kimberley worthy of being noted in this infallible source.

Now and then he and black survivors of the street marches of blacks and whites in the past get together for a drink. 'Survivors' because some of the black comrades (comrades because that form of address hadn't been exclusive to the communists among them) had moved on to high circles in cabinet posts and boardrooms. The talk turned to reform of the education system and student action to bring it about. Except for Frederick, in their shared 70s and 80s few of this group of survivors had the chance of a university education. They're not inhibited to be critical of the new regime their kind brought about or of responses to its promises unfulfilled. —Trashing the campus isn't going to scrap tuition fees for our kids too poor to pay. Yelling freedom songs, toyi-toying at the Principal's door isn't going to reach the Minister of Education's big ears. Man! Aren't there other tactics now? They're supposed to be intelligent, getting educated, not so, and all they can think of is use what we had, throw stones, trash the facilities—but the buildings and the libraries and laboratories whatnot are *theirs* now, not whitey's only—they're rubbishing what we fought for, *for* them.—

Someone asks, your department okay, no damage?

Another punctuates with a laugh. —They wouldn't touch you, no way.—

Frederick doesn't know whether to put the company right, the students don't know and if they do don't care about his actions in the past, why should they, they don't know who he *was*, the modest claim to be addressed as comrade. But that would bring another whole debate, one focused on himself.

When he got home rather late he was caught under another focus, seemed that of the eyes of the grandfatherly portrait. Or was it the mixture, first beer then whisky, unaccustomedly downed.

The Easter vacation is freedom from both work and the family kind of obligation it brought while there was marriage. Frederick did have children with the second wife but it was not his turn, in the legal conditions of access, to have the boy and girl with him for this school holiday. There were invitations from university colleagues and an attractive Italian woman he'd taken to dinner and a film recently, but he said he was going away for a break. The coast? The mountains? Kimberley.

What on earth would anyone take a break there for. If they asked, he offered, see the Big Hole, and if they didn't remember what that was he'd have reminded it was the great gouged-out mouth of the diamond pipe formation.

He had never been there and knew no-one. No-one, that was the point, the negative. The man whose eyes, whose energy of form remain open to you under glass from the generations since he lived five years here, staked his claim. One-sixteenth. There certainly are men and women, children related thicker than that in his descendant's bloodstream. The telephone directory didn't give much clue to where the cousins, collaterals, might be found living on the territory of

diamonds; assuming the addresses given with the numbers are white suburban rather than indicating areas designated under the old segregation which everywhere still bear the kind of euphemistic flowery names that disguised them and where most black and colour-mixed people, around the cities, still live. And that assumption? An old colour/class one that the level of people from whom came the girls great-grandpapa used must still be out on the periphery in the new society? Why shouldn't 'Morris, Walter J. S.' of 'Golf Course Place' be a shades-of-black who had become a big businessman owning a house where he was forbidden before and playing the game at a club he was once barred from?

Scratch a white man, Frederick Morris, and find trace of the serum of induced superiority; history never over. But while he took a good look at himself, pragmatic reasoning set him leaving the chain hotel whose atmosphere confirmed the sense of anonymity of his presence and taking roads to what were the old townships of segregation. A public holiday, so the streets, some tarred and guttered, some unsurfaced dirt with puddles floating beer cans and plastic, were cheerful racetracks of cars, taxis and buses, avoiding skittering children and men and women taking their right and time to cross where they pleased.

No-one took much notice of him. His car, on an academic's salary, was neither a newer model nor more costly make than many of those alongside, and like them being ousted from lane to lane by the occasional Mercedes with darkened windows whose owner surely should have moved by now to somesuch Golf Course Place. And as a man who went climbing at weekends and swam in the university pool early every morning since the divorce, he was sun-pigmented, not much lighter than some of the men who faced him a moment, in passing, on the streets where he walked a while as if he had a destination.

Schools were closed for the holidays, as they were for his children; he found himself at a playground. The boys were clambering the structure of the slide instead of taking the ladder, and shouting triumph as they reached the top ahead of conventional users, one lost his toe-hold and fell, howling, while the others laughed. But who could say who could have been this one that one, give or take a shade, his boy; there's simply the resemblance all boys have in their grimaces of emotion, boastful feats, agile bodies. The girls on the swings clutching younger siblings, even babies; most of them pretty but aren't all girls of the age of his daughter, pretty, though one couldn't imagine her being entrusted with a baby the way the mothers sitting by placidly allowed this. The mothers. The lucky ones (favoured by prospectors?) warm honey-coloured, the others dingy between black and white, as if determined by an under-exposed photograph. Genes the developing agent. Which of these could be a Morris, a long-descended sister-cousin, whatever, alive, we're together here in the present. Could you give me a strand of your hair (his own is lank and straight but that proves nothing after the Caucasian blood mixtures of so many following progenitors) to be matched with my toe-nail cutting or a shred of my skin in DNA tests. Imagine the reaction when I handed in these to the laboratories at the university. Faculty laughter to cover embarrassment, curiosity. Fred behaving oddly nowadays.

He ate a *boerewors* roll at a street barrow, asking for it in the language, Afrikaans, that was being spoken all around him.

Their mother tongue, the girls who visited the old man spoke (not old then, no, all the vital juices flowing, showing); did he pick it up from them and promptly forget it in London and Amsterdam as he did them, never came back to Africa. He, the descendant, hung on in the township until late afternoon, hardly knowing the object of lingering, or leaving. Then there were bars filling up behind men talking at the entrances against kwaito music. He made his way into one and took a bar stool warm from the backside of the man who swivelled off it. After a beer the voices and laughter, the beat of the music made him feel strangely relaxed on this venture of his he didn't try to explain to himself that began before the convex glass of the oval-framed photograph. When his neighbour, whose elbow rose and fell in dramatic gestures to accompany a laughing bellowing argument, jolted and spilled the foam of the second beer, the interloper grinned, gave assurances of no offence taken and was drawn into friendly banter with the neighbour and his pals. The argument was about the referee's decision in a soccer game; he'd played when he was a student and could contribute a generalised opinion of the abilities, or lack of, among referees. In the pause when the others called for another round, including him without question, he was able to ask (it was suddenly remembered) did anyone know a Morris family living around? There were self-questioning raised foreheads, they looked to one another: one moved his head slowly side to side, down over the dregs in his glass; drew up from it, when I was a kid, another kid . . . his people moved to another section, they used to live here by the church.

Alternative townships were suggested. Might be people with that name there. So did he know them from somewhere? Wha'd'you want them for?

It came quite naturally. They're family we've lost touch with.

Oh that's how it is people go all over, you never hear what's with them, these days, it's let's try this place let's try that and you never know they's alive or dead, my brothers gone off to Cape Town they don't know who they are anymore . . . so where you from?

From the science faculty of the university with the classical columns, the progeny of men and women in the professions, generations of privilege that have made them whatever it is they are. They don't know what they might have been.

Names, unrecorded on birth certificates—if there were any such for the issue of foreign prospectors' passing sexual relief—get lost, don't exist, maybe abandoned as worthless. These bar-room companions buddies comrades, could any one of them be men who should have my family name included in theirs?

So where am I from.

What was it all about.

Dubious. What kind of claim do you *need*? The standard of privilege changes with each regime. Isn't it a try at privilege. Yes? One up towards the ruling class whatever it may happen to be. One-sixteenth. A cousin how many times removed from the projection of your own male needs onto the handsome young buck preserved under glass. So what's happened to the ideal of the Struggle (the capitalised generic of something else that's never over, never mind history-book victories) for recognition, beginning in the self, that our kind, humankind, doesn't need any distinctions of blood percentage tincture. That fucked things up enough in the past. Once there were blacks, poor devils, wanting to claim white. Now there's a white, poor devil, wanting to claim black. It's the same secret.

His colleagues in the faculty coffee room at the university exchange Easter holiday pleasures, mountains climbed, animals in a game reserve, the theatre, concerts—and one wryly confessing: trying to catch up with reading for the planning of a new course, sustained by warm beer consumed in the sun.

—Oh and how was the Big Hole?—

—Deep.—

Everyone laughs at witty deadpan brevity.

tape measure

NO-ONE of any kind or shape or species can begin to imagine what it's like for me being swirled and twisted around all manner of filthy objects in a horrible current. I, who was used to, knew only, the calm processes of digestion as my milieu. How long will this chaos last (the digestion has its ordained programme) and where am I going? Helpless. All I can do is trace back along my length—it is considerable also in the measure of its time—how I began and lived and what has happened to me.

My beginning is ingestion—yes, sounds strange. But there it is. I might have been ingested on a scrap of lettuce or in a delicacy of raw minced meat known as, I believe, Beefsteak Tartare. Could have got in on a finger licked by my human host after he'd ignored he'd been caressing his dog or cat. Doesn't matter. Once I'd been ingested I knew what to do where I found myself, I gained consciousness; nature is a miracle in the know-how it has provided, ready, in all its millions of varieties of eggs: I hatched from my minute containment that the human eye never could have detected on the lettuce, the raw meat, the finger, and began to grow myself. Segment by segment. Measuredly. That's how my species adapts and maintains itself, advances to feed along one of the most intricately designed passageways in the world. An organic one. Of course, that's connected with perhaps an even more intricate system, the whole business of veins and arteries—bloody; our species has nothing to do with that pulsing about all over in narrow tubes.

My place was warm and smooth-walled, rosy-dark, and down into its convolutions (around thirty coiled feet of it) came, sometimes more regularly than others, always ample, many different kinds of nourishment to feed on, silently, unknown and unobserved. An ideal existence! The many forms of life, in particular that of millions of the species of my host who go hungry in the cruel light and cold my darkness protected me from (with the nourishment comes not only what the host eats but intelligence of what he knows of his kind's being and environment)—they would envy one of my kind. No enemy, no predator after you, no rival. Just your own winding length, moving freely, resting sated. The nourishment that arrived so reliably—years and years in my case—was even already broken down for consumption, ready mashed, you might say, and mixed with sustaining liquids. Sometimes during my long habitation there would be a descent of some potent liquid that roused me pleasurably all my length—which, as I've remarked had become considerable—so that I was lively, so to speak, right down to the last, most recently-added segments of myself.

Come to think of it, there were a couple of attempts on my

life before the present catastrophe. But they didn't succeed.
No! I detected at once, infallibly, some substance *aggressive* towards me concealed in the nourishment coming down. Didn't
touch that delivery. Let it slowly urge its way wherever it was
going—in its usual pulsions, just as when I have had my fill;
untouched! No thank you. I could wait until the next delivery
came down: clean, I could tell. Whatever my host had in
mind, then, I was my whole length aware, ahead of him. Yes!
Oh and there was one occurence that might or might not have
had to do with whatever this aggression against my peaceful
existence might mean. My home, my length, were suddenly
irradiated with some weird seconds-long form of what I'd
learnt second-hand from my host must have been light, as if
some—Thing—was briefly enabled to look inside my host.
All the wonderful secret storage that was my domain. But did
those rays find me? See me? I didn't think so. All was undis-
turbed, for me, for a long time. I continued to grow myself,
perfectly measured segment by segment. Didn't brood upon
the brief invasion of my privacy; I have a calm nature, like all
my kind. Perhaps I should have thought more about the incident's implication: that thereafter my host *knew I was there*; the
act of ingestion conveys nothing about what's gone down with
the scrap of lettuce or the meat: he wouldn't have been aware
of my residency until then. But suspected something? How,
I'd like to know; I was so discreet.

The gouts of that agreeable strong liquid began to reach
me more frequently. No objection on my part! The stuff just
made me more active for a while, I had grown to take up a lot
of space in my domain, and I have to confess that I would find
myself inclined to ripple and knock about a bit. Harmlessly, of

course. We don't have voices so I couldn't sing. Then there would follow a really torpid interval of which I'd never remember much when it was over . . .

A contented, shared life; I knew that my host had always taken what he needed from the nourishment that came on down to me. A just and fair coexistence, I still maintain. And why should I have troubled myself with where the residue was bound for, when both of us had been satisfied?

O HOW I have come to know now! How I have come to know!

For what has just happened to me—I can only relive again, again, in all horror, as if it keeps recurring all along me. First there was that period, quite short, when no nourishment or liquid came down at all. My host must have been abstaining.

Then—

The assault of a terrible flood, bitter burning, whipping and pursuing all down and around into a pitch-black narrow passage filled with stinking filth. I've become part of what is pushing its path there—*that* was where the nourishment was bound for all the years, after the host and I had done with it, a suffocating putrifaction and unbearable effusions.

Jonah was spewed by the whale.

But I—the term for it, I believe—was shat out.

From that cess I've been ejected into what was only a more spacious one, round, hard-surfaced, my segments have never touched against anything like it, in my moist-padded soft home space, and I am tossed along with more and many, many kinds of rottenness, objects, sections of which I sense from my own completeness must be dismembered from organic wholes

that one such as myself, who has never before known the outside, only the insides of existence, cannot name. Battered
through this conduit by these forms, all ghastly, lifeless, I
think I must somehow die among them—I have the knowledge how to grow but not how to die if, as it seems, that is
necessary. And now! Now! The whole putrid torrent had
somewhere it was bound for—it discharges (there is a moment's blinding that must be light) and disperses into a vol-
ume of liquid inconceivable in terms of the trickles and even
gouts that had fed me. Unfathomable: I am swept up in something heady, frothy, exhilarating; down with something that
flows me. And I am clean, clean the whole length of me! Ah to
be cleansed of that filth I had never suspected was what the
nourishment I shared with my host became when we'd taken
our fill of it. Blessed ignorance, all those years I was safe inside . . .

My host. So *he* knew. This's how he planned to get rid of
me. Why? What for? This's how he respected our coexistence,
after even sharing with me those gouts of agreeable liquid
whose happy effects we must have enjoyed together. It ends
up, him driving me out mercilessly, hatefully, with every kind
of ordure. Deadly.

BUT I'm adapting to this vastness! Can, at least, for a
while, I believe. It's not what I was used to and there's no
nourishment of my habitude but I find that my segments, the
entire length of me still obeys; I can progress by my normal
undulation. Undulating, I'm setting out in an element that
also does, I'm setting out for what this powerful liquid vastness is bound for—nature's built into my knowledge that

everything has to move somewhere—and maybe there, where this force lands, one of my eggs (we all have a store within us, although we are loners and our fertilisation is a secret) will find a housefly carrier and settle on a scrap of lettuce or a fine piece of meat in a Beefsteak Tartare. Ingestion. The whole process shall begin over again. Come to life.

dreaming of the dead

DID you come back last night?

I try to dream you into materialisation but you don't appear.

I keep expecting you. Because dream has no place, time. The Empyrean—always liked that as my free-floating definition of Somenowhere—balloon without tether to earth. There is no past no present no future. All is occupied at once. Everyone there is without boundaries of probability.

I don't know why it was a Chinese restaurant—ah, no, the choice is going to come clear later when a particular one of the guests arrives! Guests? Whose invitation is it. Who hosts. Such causation doesn't apply; left behind. Look up and there's Edward, the coin-clear profile of Edward Said that is aware how masculinely beautiful it still exists in photographs, he's turning this way and that to find where the table is that expects him. It's his decision it's this one. He's always known what was meant for him, the placing of himself, by himself, through the path of any obstacles, Christian-Muslim, Palestinian-Cairene,

American. He's his own usher, shining a torch of distinctive intellectual light and sensibility to guide him. It's not the place to remember this, here, but if you're the one still living in the flesh wired up by synapses and neurons you recall his wife Mariam told that on his last journey to the hospital he disputed the route taken by the driver.

Edward. He stands a moment, before the embrace of greeting. His familiar way of marking the event of a meeting brought about by the co-ordination of friends' commitments and lucky happenstance. It's reassuring he's wearing one of the coloured shirts and the flourished design of his tie is confirmed by the ear of a silk handkerchief showing above the breast pocket of the usual elegant jacket. Edward never needed to prove his mental superiority by professorial dowdiness and dandruff. We don't bother with how-are-yous, there's no point in that sort of banality, here. He says why don't we have a drink while we're waiting—he seems to know for whom although I don't (except, for you) any more than I knew he would come to this place hung with fringed paper lanterns. He beckons a waiter who doesn't pretend in customary assertion of dignity against servility that he hasn't noticed. Edward never had to command, I'd often noted that, there is something in those eyes fathomless black with ancient Middle Eastern ancestry, that has no need of demanding words. With the glance back to me, he orders what we've always drunk to being well-met. He apologises with humour 'I don't know how I managed to be late, it's quite an art' though he isn't late because he never was expected, and there can be no explanation I could understand of what could have kept him.

We plunge right away into our customary eager exchange of interpretations of political events, international power-

mongering, national religious and secular conflicts, the obses-
sional scaffolding of human existence on earth, then ready
to turn to personal preoccupations, for which, instinctively
selected in each friendship, there is a different level of confidences. Before we get to ours, someone else arrives at our
table; even I, who have known that face in its changes over
many years and in relation to many scenes and circumstances,
from treason trials in the country where I am still one of the
living, to all-night parties in London, don't recognise his entry. Once standing at this table, the face creased in his British
laugh of greeting: it's Anthony Sampson. Who? Because instead of the baggy pants unworthy of tweed jacket, he's wearing an African robe. Not just a dashiki shirt he might have
picked up on his times in Africa, and donned for comfortable
summer informality of whatever this gathering is, but a robe
to the ankles—by the way, it can't be hot in the Chinese
restaurant; there's no climate in dream. When he was editor of
a black-staffed newspaper in South Africa and belonged, was
an intimate of shebeen ghettos, never mind his pink British
skin, this preceded the era when African garb became fashionable as a mark of the wearer's non-racism. Sampson had no interest in being fashionable within any convention. He showed
no consciousness, now, of his flowing robe. So neither did I;
nor did Edward though I suppose they had met in the Elsewhere. Edward rose while Anthony and I hugged, kissed
on either cheek, he greeted Edward with recollected—it
seemed—admiration and chose a chair, having to arrange the
robe out of the way of his shoes, like a skirt.

We took up, three of us now, the interrupted talk of political conflict and scandals, policies and ideologies, corrupt gov-
ernments, tyrant fundamentalists, homegrown in the Middle

East and Eastern Europe, and those created by the hubris of the West. A waiter subserviently intruded with distributed menus but we all ignored him as if it were understood we were waiting for someone. I was waiting for you. Even in that Chinese restaurant though it was never your favourite cuisine.

Whom were we waiting for?

I wonder now, awakened in bed by a heavy cat settling on my feet, but I didn't then, no-one asked me so I didn't have to give my answer: you. Edward opened a menu big and leather-bound as a book of world maps. Perhaps this meant he and Anthony knew no-one was coming. No-one else was available among the dead in their circle. Maybe the too newly-dead cannot enter dreams. But no; Anthony was recent, and here he was, if strangely got up in the category of the childhood belief that when you die you grow wings, become angels in the Empyrean.

Suddenly she was there, sitting at the head of the table as if she had been with us all along or because there was no time we hadn't remarked when it was she'd joined us. Susan. Susan Sontag. How to have missed the doorway entrance of that presence always larger-than-life (stupid metaphor to have chosen in the circumstances, but this is a morning-after account) not only in sense of her height and size: a mythical goddess, Athena-Medea statue with that magnificent head of black hair asserting this doubling authority, at once inspiring, menacing, unveiling a sculptor's bold marble features, gouged by commanding eyes.

It seemed there had been greetings. Exclamations of pleasure, embraces and less intimate but just as sincere pressures of hands left animation, everyone talking at once across one another. Susan's deep beautiful voice interrupted itself in an aside to call a waiter by name—well of course, so this is the Chinese restaurant in New York's SoHo she used to take me to! The waiters know her, she's the habituée who judges what's particularly good to order, in fact she countermands with an affectionate gesture of a fine hand the hesitant choices of the others and questions, insists, laughs reprovingly at some of the waiter's suggestions; he surely is aware of what the cooks can't get away with, with her. She does let us decide on what to drink. Susan was never a drinker and this one among her favourite eating places probably doesn't have a cellar of the standard that holds the special French and Italian cultivars for which she makes an exception.

As if, non-smoker, she carries a box of matches, there strikes from her a flame flaring the Israeli-Palestinian situation. The light's turned on Edward, naturally, although this is not a group in which each sees personal identity and its supposed unquestioning loyalty cast by birth, faith, country, race, as the decisive and immutable sum of self. Edward is a Palestinian, he's also in his ethics of human being, a Jew, we know that from his writings, his exposure of the orientalism within us, the invention of the Other that's survived the end of the old-style colonialism into globalisation. If Susan's a Jew, she too, has identity beyond that label, hers has been one with Vietnamese, Sarajevans, many others, to make up the sum of self.

They carry all this to the Somenowhere. In the Chinese restaurant, there between us.

Sampson doesn't interject much in that understated rapidity of half-audible upperclass English delivery, yet gives a new twist to what's emerging from the other two eloquently contesting one another from different points of view even on what they agree upon. A journalist who's achieved distinction of complete integrity in venturous success must have begun by being a good listener. And I—my opinions and judgments are way down in the confusion of living, I don't have the perspective the dead must have attained. But the distance with which Edward seems to regard Susan's insistent return to passionate views of opposing legitimacies between Palestinians and Israelis is puzzling. After all his clarity and commitment on that conflict-trampled ground of the earth he's left behind, searching the unambiguous words and taking the actions for a just resolution (on the premise there is one), putting his brilliant mind to it against every hostility, including the last—death: how this lack of response? Lassitude? Is that the peace of the dead that passeth all understanding the public relations spin doctors of religions advertise? The hype by one to counter that other, a gratis supply of virgins? Lassitude. But Edward Said: never an inactive cell in that unique brain.

'What did you leave unfinished?'

The favoured waiter had wheeled to the table a double-deck buffet almost the table's length, displaying a composition of glistening mounds, gardens of bristling greens. Susan with her never sated search for truth rather than being fobbed off with information, dared to introduce as she turned to the food's array, a subject it perhaps isn't done to raise among the other guests.

She was helping herself with critical concentration, this, no, then that—and some more of that—filling to her satisfaction, aesthetic and anticipatory, the large plates the restaurant earned its reputation by providing.

Edward waited for her to reach this result. 'Everything is unfinished. Finality: that's the mistake. It's the claim of dictatorship. Hegemony. In our turn, always we'll be having to pick up the baggage taking from experience what's good, discarding what's conned us into prizing, if it's destructive.'

Dream has no sequence as we know it, this following that. This over, that beginning. You can be making love with someone unrecognised, picking up coins spilled in the street, giving a speech at a board meeting, pursued naked in a shopping mall, without the necessary displacements of sequence. Whether the guests were serving themselves—the others, Anthony and Edward—and whether they were talking between mouthfuls and those swallows of wine or water which precede what one's going to say at table, I was mistaken in my logic of one still living, that they were continuing their exchange of the responsibilities for 9/11, the Tsunami, famine in Darfur, elections in Iraq, the Ukraine, student riots against youth employment restrictions in Paris, a rape charge in court indicting a member of government in my country: preoccupations of my own living present or recent months, years; naturally all one to them. What was I doing there in Susan's Chinese restaurant, anyway?

It is news they're exchanging of what they're engaged in. Now. Edward's being urged to tell something that at least explains to me his certain distance from Susan's perceptions of the developments (at whatever stage these might have been when she left access to newspapers, television, inside informants) in the Middle East. He's just completed a piano concerto. I can't resist putting in with delight 'For two pianos.' The Said apartment on the Upper West Side in New York had what you'd never expect to walk in on, two grand pianos taking up one of the livingrooms. Edward once remarked to me, if affectionately, 'You have the writing but I have the writing and the music.' An amateur pianist of concert performance level, he'd played with an orchestra under the baton of his friend Daniel Barenboim.

Here was his acknowledging smile of having once led me into that exotically furnished livingroom; maybe a brush of his hand. Touch isn't always felt, in dream. There was a scholar, a politico-philosophical intellect, an enquirer of international morality in the order of the world, a life whose driving motivation was not chosen but placed upon him: Palestinian. An existential destiny, among his worldly others. It's cast in the foundations, the academic chairs, honours endowed in the name. All that. But death's the discarder he didn't mention. Edward Said is a composer. There's also the baggage you do take. Two grand pianos. Among the living, it's Carlos Fuentes who asks if music is not the 'true fig leaf of our shames, the final sublimation—beyond death—of our mortal visibility: body of words'. Is only music 'free of visible ties, the purification and illusions of our bodily misery'?

Edward. A composer. What he always was, should have been; but there was too much demand upon him from the threatening outer world? It's a symphony Edward Said's working on now.

'What's the theme, what are you giving us?' Susan is never afraid to be insistent, her passion for all creation so strong this justifies intrusion.

'I don't have to tell you that the movements of a symphony are in sum just that, a resolution, symphonically.' Edward is paying an aside tribute to her non-performer's love and knowledge of music. 'It's still—what should I say—'

'You hear it, you play it? It's in your fingers?' Susan is re-

lentless in pursuit of the process, from one who's been an elo-
quent man of words people haven't always wanted to hear.

He lifts his shoulders and considers. Doesn't she know
that's the way, equivalent of scribbled phrases, jotted half-
sentences, essential single words spoken into a recording
gadget, which preceded the books she's written, the books he
wrote. The symphony he's—hearing? playing? transposing to
the art's hieroglyphics?—it's based on Jewish folk songs and
Palestinian laments or chants.

Ours is a choir of enthusiasm. When will the work be completed. How far along realised. 'It's done' Edward says. Ready.
'For the orchestra' and spreads palms and forearms wide from
elbows pressed at his sides. I read his mind as the dreamer can:
just unfortunate Barenboim can't be ready to conduct the
work; isn't here yet.

These are people who are accustomed to being engaged by
the directions taken by one another, ideas, thought and action.
No small table talk. Anthony Sampson takes the opportunity,
simply because he hasn't before been able to acknowledge to
Susan she shamed the complacent acceptance of suffering as
no-one else has done. Since Goya!

Susan gives her splendid congratulatory, deprecatory laugh,
and in response quotes what confronts TV onlookers 'still in
Time, the pictures will not go away: that is the nature of the
digital world'. Not long dead, she hasn't quite vacated it: this
comes from one of her last looks at the world, the book which
Anthony is praising, *Regarding the Pain of Others.*

But that's for the memory museum left behind as if it were
the phenomenon that, for a while, the hair of the dead continues to grow. Susan has brought with her the sword of words

she has always flashed skilfully in defence of the disarmed. She's taken up the defence of men.

'You!' Edward appreciates what surely will be a new style of feminist foil. We're all laughing anticipation. But Susan Sontag is no Quixote, wearing a barber's basin as the helmet of battledress.

'What has made them powerless to live fully? Never mind Huntington and his clash of civilisations. The clash of the sexes has brought about subjection of the heterosexual male. We women have achieved the last result, surely, as emancipated beings, we wanted? A reversal of roles of oppressor and oppressed, the demeaning of fellow humans. Affirmative action has created a gender elite which behaves as the male one did, high positions for pals just as the men awarded whether the individual was or was not qualified except by what was between the legs.'

Someone—might have been I—said, 'Muslim women—still behind the black veil—men suffer from them.' It's taken as rhetorical.

I'm no match for Susan.

'See them trailing the wives and mothers grandmothers matriarchs aunts sisters along with endless children: that's the power behind the burka. *Their* men—don't forget the possessive—carry the whole female burden through entire male lives, bearing women who know that to come out and fend for yourself means competing economically, politically, psychologically in the reality of the world. The black rag's an iron curtain.'

'And gay men?' Anthony's a known lover of women but his sense of justice is alert and quizzical as anyone's.

Susan looks him over: maybe she's mistaken his obvious

heterosexuality, his confidence that he's needed no defence in his relations with females. She's addressing us all.

'When the gay bar closes, it's the lesbians who get the jobs—open to their gender *as women*. Gay men aren't even acceptable for that last resort of traditional male *amour propre*, the army, in many countries. Unfit even to be slaughtered.'

Meanwhile Edward's found his appetite, he's considering this dish, then that, in choice of which promises the subtlety that appeals to him as (oh unworthy comparison I'm making) he might consider between the performance of one musician and another at the piano. As the left hand pronounces a chord and the right hand answers higher. But the discrimination of taste buds' pleasures does not temper his demand, 'What's happened to penis envy?'

Nevertheless, Susan gives him the advice he clearly needs, not duck, the prawns are better, no, no, that chicken concoction is for dull palates.

The waiter is already swaying servilely this way and that with a discreet offer of the dessert menu; some of us have done with the main spread. Maybe we're ready for what I remember comes next in this place which is just as it was, the trolleys of bounty will never empty. Fortune cookies. Sorbet with litchis; mangoes? Perhaps it's the names of tropical fruits that remind us of Anthony's form of dress. 'What are you up to?' It's Edward. 'Whose international corporate anatomy are you dissecting.' As if the African robe must be some kind of journalist surgeon's operating garb. Oracular Edward recalls, 'Who would have foreseen even the most powerful in the world come to fear of running dry—except you, of course, when you wrote your *Seven Sisters* . . . that was . . .' The readers of his book about the oil industry, the writer himself, ignore reference to the memory museum, its temporal documentation. 'Who foresaw it was those oilfields witches' brew that fuels the world which was going to be more pricey than gold, platinum, uranium, yes! —Yes!—in terms of military strategy for power, the violent grab for spheres of supply, never mind political influence. Who saw it was going to be guns for oil, blood for oil. *You did!*'

I don't know at what stage the continuing oil crisis exists in the awareness of the Chinese restaurant Empyrean.

Anthony is shrugging and laughing embarrassedly under an accolade. Now—forever—he's proved prophet but there's only the British tribe's understatement, coming from him. 'Anybody could have known it.'

Susan takes up with her flourish, Edward's imagery. 'Double, double, toil and trouble, the cauldron that received what gushed from earth and seabed? They didn't.'

Edward and Susan enjoy Sampson's modesty, urging him on.

'Well, if the book should—could—might have been somehow . . .' Dismissing bent tilt of head.

Of course, who knows if hindsight's seeing it reprinted, best-selling. There's no use for royalties anyway. No tariff for the Chinese lunch.

Now it's Susan who presses. 'So what're you up to.'

Maybe he's counting that Mandela will arrive soon, so he can add an afterword to his famous biography of the great man.

'Oh it'd be good to see you sometime at the tavern.'

Tavern?

Probably I'm the only one other than Sampson himself who knows that's the South African politically correct term for what used to be black ghetto shebeens (old term second-hand from the Irish).

Susan turns down her beautiful mouth generously shaped for disbelief and looks to Edward. The wells of his gaze send back from depths, reflection of shared intrigue.

Anthony Sampson has some sort of bar.

Did he add 'my place'—that attractive British secretive mumble always half-audible. So that would explain the African dress. And yet make it more of a mystery to us (if, the dreamer, I'm not one of those summoned up, can be included in the dream).

'How long has this place been going?' Susan again.

Where?

Where isn't relevant. There's no site, just as with the Chinese restaurant conjured up by Susan's expectation of her arrival. (Couldn't have been a place of my expectation of you.)

How long?

The African garment isn't merely a comfortable choice for what might have been anticipated as an overheated New York–style restaurant. It is a ritual accoutrement, a professional robe. Anthony Sampson has spent some special kind of attention, since there is no measure by time, in induction as a sangoma.

Sangoma. What. *What* is that.

I know it's what's commonly understood as a 'witch doctor', but that's an imperio-colonialist term neither of Anthony's companions would want to use, particularly not Edward, whose classic work *Orientalism* is certainly still running into many editions as evidence of the avatars of the old power phenomenon in guise under new names.

Sampson's 'place' is a shebeen which was part of his place in

Africa that was never vacated by him when he went back to England, as the Chinese restaurant is part of her place, never vacated in Susan's New York. But the shebeen seems put to a different purpose; or rather carries in its transformation what really had existed there already. Sampson's not one in a crowd and huddle that always made itself heard above the music in 'The House of Truth'—ah, that was the name in the Sophiatown 'slum' of the white city, poetic in such claims for its venues. He's not just one of the swallowers of a Big Mama's concoction of beer-brandy-brakefluid, Godknowswhat, listening to, entering the joys, sorrows, moods defiant and despairing, brazenly alive, of men and women who made him a brother there.

He has returned to this, to something of the world, from isolation in the bush of Somenowhere with knowledge to offer instead of, as bar proprietor, free drinks. The knowledge of the traditional healer. He serves the sangoma's diagnoses of and alleviations of the sorrows, defiances and despairs that can't be drowned or danced, sung away together.

'Oh a shrink!'

Who would have thought Susan, savant of many variations of cultures, could be so amazed. The impact throws back her splendid head in laughter.

At 'Tony's Place', his extraordinary gifts as a journalist elevated to another sphere of inquiry, he guides with the third eye his bar patrons—wait a minute; his patients—to go after what's behind their presented motives of other people, and what's harmful behind the patient's own. He dismisses: doesn't make love potions. Hate potions to sprinkle, deadly, round a rival's house? That's witch doctor magic, not healing. The patrons, beer in hand, talk to him, talk out the inner self. As he reluctantly continues to recount, he says that he observes their body language, he gathers what lies unconfessed between the words. No. He doesn't tell them what to do, dictate a solution to confound, destroy the enemy, he directs them to deal with themselves.

'A psychotherapist! Oh of course, that's it. Dear Anthony!' He's proved psychotherapy was first practised in ancient Africa, like so many Western 'discoveries' claimed by the rest of the world. Susan puts an arm round his shoulders to recognise him as an original.

And aren't they, all three. How shall we do without them? They're drifting away, they're leaving the table, I hear in the archive of my head broken lines from adolescent reading, an example that fits Edward's definition of Western orientalism, some European's version of the work of an ancient Persian poet. It's not the bit about the jug of wine and thou. '. . . Some we loved, the loveliest and the best . . . Have drunk their cup a round or two before / And one by one crept silently to rest.' Alone in the Chinese restaurant, it comes to me not as exotic romanticism but as the departure of the three guests.

I sat at the table, you didn't turn up, too late.

You will not come. Never.

a frivolous woman

WHEN she died they found in an old cabin trunk elaborate as a pirate's chest a variety of masquerade costumes, two sequinned masks, and folders protecting dinner menus flourished with witty drawings dedicated by the artists.

She had brought the treasure trove from Berlin as a refugee from Nazi extermination of Jewish Germans. She left behind, dispossessed of, the fine house where the dinners were given, the guests famous opera singers, orchestra conductors, painters, art collectors and Weimar Republic politicians—Walter Rathenau, the Liberal last Minister of Foreign Affairs in that government, a regular at table, had been assassinated by Right Wing radicals.

Her family in the country of emigration lifted this cache forty years later, laughing, shaking heads, grimacing incredulity. One of the adult grandsons, for whom she was history, thought but did not speak: she rescued this junk to bring along while others like her were transported in cattle trucks.

Old Grete! Her son would tell how at party gatherings in

the adoptive country to which he had gained entry for himself, his wife and mother, he was as a young man embarrassed when she would disappear to another room briefly and reappear in the doorway, castanets and mantilla, singing and stamping as Carmen. But he must have been habituated *in utero* to her gregarious flair for performance, because the night of his birth is celebrated on a poster announcing the opening of an exhibition of paintings by the Impressionist Lovis Corinth at a fashionable Berlin gallery; confident that with a second pregnancy she could calculate the progression of birth-pains, his mother had said nothing about them and accompanied her husband to an occasion she would never allow herself to miss, a *vernissage*. On arrival back home, she delivered the boy. The story is verified by his birth certificate (among emigration papers) and the reproduction of the poster in an art book.

What her son didn't tell was the other story of her emigration. The Carmen act, which many people found part of their heightened party mood, was significant in that she had at the same time settled in a boardinghouse apparently without remarking comparison with the elegant rooms that now housed some Third Reich official. But in 1939 she insisted, against her son's vociferous objections, on going back to Europe. How could she abandon Heinrich! She must visit her elder son, who had chosen Denmark. Unlike his intelligently foresighted young brother, he was one of those who wanted to be nearby because the Hitler episode surely couldn't last. She concealed from the son who had managed to bring her safely to a country far enough distant, that she was also going back to Berlin. She couldn't abandon either, the wonderful old family retainers—not Jews, fortunately for them—the faithful gardener-handyman inherited from her own father, the peasant woman who had been wet-nurse and nanny to the children and stayed on in some undefined capacity in what was her only life. And of course, friends in the old cultured set who, like the humble kind of retainers were securely not Jews—and would never be Nazis? She was apparently blithely unaware that she might compromise them by claiming long friendship; her family had been assimilated for generations. They enjoyed pork like any good German and didn't circumcise their sons.

When her letters started to come post-marked Germany her son demanded she leave at once. She lingered with cajoling, reassuring excuses—just another week, what's the difference. At last she took ship in Holland, emigrating a second time from the same Rotterdam on the same line. Three days at sea: the news that war was declared between Britain and Germany. What was to be the Second World War had begun. When the ship reached Senegal on the West Coast of Africa, it was impounded at the port of Dakar. Senegal was a French colony and France, by then, had entered the war as Britain's ally. The truant mother still held a German passport and along with others who did, she was taken under guard from the ship to detention at a camp in the ruin of a leper asylum outside the city. Her son expected her to arrive at a port in their adopted country on a scheduled date. Holland had not declared war, there was no reason that a ship of the Holland Afrika Line would be hampered on its route. He arranged for a friend to meet his mother when she disembarked and see her onto a train bound for home upcountry, where he was awaiting her. Instead there came an incoherent frantic call from the friend. The ship had docked, passengers emerged, but Grete did not. There were relatives and friends ready to greet returning travellers who also waited in bewilderment as these did not come waving happily down the gangplank. Everyone sought an explanation from somebody, anybody. Out of the clamour at last the Captain appeared and as if still stunned by fear told that he could do nothing when the French authorities boarded his ship and demanded to take German passport holders into custody. He did not know where they were held.

There began for the son what must have been a nightmare both surreal and desperately practical. He has somewhere stowed—what does one do this for?—in the cache of *his* documented life, the letters, the official rejections, the notes of imploring visits to consulates and government departments in strategy to get her released.

If she were still alive.

How could bureaucratic processes—only ones available, badgering the Red Cross, importuning the aghast Swedes who hastily had been made the representatives of people detained in makeshift camps God knows how where by the chaos of war—reach the void, silence; worse, a gust of images tossing up thirst, hunger, parched desert, tropical deluge.

After three weeks there was a letter. The headed address: Camp de Concentration de Sébikholane. Alive: her flowing hand on a dirty piece of paper. Her English. Many exclamation marks following the announcement that because she speaks French she has been able to persuade a guard to mail the letter. She has had fever but it's quite okay now. The other people with her are wonderful. There's a circus troupe and she's great pals with them; the trapeze girl has a bed next to hers in the tent where everyone sleeps, and so her boy-friend, also from the high wire, comes to her, so sweet, I just put up my umbrella that side of my bed. I know, darling son, you are doing everything what's for sure to get me out of here. There are big rats! It is terribly hot but they say that in a few weeks will be cooler.

A postcript. Everyone is so pleased because I've also got the French guard to bring us each a quarter litre of red wine a day!

The Red Cross, French Consulate, bewildered Swedes somehow succeeded; after six weeks the inhabitants of the camp were released to complete their journey on the Holland Afrika Line. She opened her arms to her son just the way she had always done when he was a boy and she returned from Deauville or a spa in Switzerland. And as herself a child who charms with the assumption that all is forgiven she showed no contrition for the anxiety and dread she had caused by her naughty escapade. Anger and frustration had battled with fear, in her son, and fear had won—how could he reproach her. Looking instead for what might have been part of the reason for his mother taking off against his edict, he thought to install her in a comfortable apartment with a daily maid, but she had her way with her usual style of retort, staying on in the boardinghouse: Where else I can live where I'm the youngest?

For old Grete everything was a party. At least he persuaded her to have a health check with one of her boardinghouse *salon* habitués, an immigrant doctor from Frankfurt. He confirmed that the fever symptoms he asked her to recollect were indeed those of malaria, and the virus might be sleeping in her blood, to recur with another bout. She chose to misunderstand. '*Ach Kwatsch!* I sleep like a baby.' It was true that in her cubby-hole room she kept to her divisions of time decided long ago in the style of Berlin high life—never in bed until after midnight and never up before noon. From this came one of the impossible old Grete incidents. The room did not have an adjoining private bathroom, she trailed sociably in flounced dressing-gown and flowered plastic mobcap to a communal one. There was only a hand-basin with running water in the room. The boardinghouse also did not employ maids; it was usual in those years for 'bedroom boys' to serve instead. The grown men, black, came from rural areas and were issued with a garb of coarse white cotton shorts that mimicked the baggy khaki ones of early British settlers. She chatted with her elderly 'bedroom boy', and had secretly arranged with him to come quietly into her room and fulfil his cleaning duties while she was asleep, since she rose long after his morning round was supposed to be completed. This was something else to be concealed, this time from the boardinghouse proprietor, both for the employee's sake and her own. She opened her eyes one morning and saw the bedroom boy watching himself in the mirror while brushing his bared teeth with her toothbrush. When told to amuse him, her son also drew back lips, bared teeth, in incredulous distaste: what did she intend to do about it? She had bought a toothbrush and presented—Here is yours, Josiah.

Her social life, like her time, was constructed in accordance with its diminished scale on the old model she knew. No post-opera parties—not much opera around—concerts and, of course, nightclubs. As dancing partners she had her one or two regulars. They were homosexuals (gay was not yet a mood exclusive to gender), therefore not gigolos, with sexual obligations. They were not paid; just younger immigrants in her set who missed partying as she did and for which, less impecunious than they, she paid. She also picked up as other friends people with whom her son and the family wouldn't have thought she would have anything in common, just as they wouldn't. A bustling talkative Afrikaner woman, The Pienaar (these useful women were referred to in the definitive by their surnames), perhaps began as someone paid for small services, fetching clothes from the dry cleaners', sewing on buttons, and then stayed for coffee and cake. There was an Italian or was it a Portuguese pickup, young, who sold tickets at a cinema— with her married lover she was invited to threesome dinners. When Marlene Dietrich on the final-appearance world tour that famous actors and musicians are reduced to in their decline, came to Africa, the sister-Berliner who had idolised the unique voice and incomparable legs, treated the family to a performance. The family saw another old lady up on stage, whom the grandmother with the same raggedly-red painted mouth as the singer jumped to cheer emotionally as they did live appearances of pop stars. But old Grete's love of celebrity did not belong back in the past. The adrenalin worked even for current sports heroes in the adopted country, and certain political figures, General Jan Smuts, as it had for Walter Rathenau. Grandmother is a groupie. As there are playboys, she must be accepted for herself, a playgirl.

What was banished was much; quite other. What could not make a good story to entertain, draw on light-hearted liveliness, was not admitted for communication. Foreign to her nature. Although they had lived through devastating events together in their life, back there, she and her son never talked of them to one another, nor, for relief, in private confession to others; evidently she imposed this self-practice to be respected by him. His father, her husband, had died at fifty when the boy was twelve. Apparently she felt no need to return to what the loss must have meant to them, together and differently. The son learnt by chance, later, that his father had had an affair with an intellectual, a woman among their familiars, that ended only when he suddenly became ill and died. His mother had known; but the only reference that could be traced to this was that sometimes, describing the company recalled at splendid social occasions she mentioned mischievously, by name, the usual presence of the woman whom, she added, she and her sister knew as *'Die Bärin'*, the She-bear, unfemininely hairy.

His mother married again when he was eighteen and his brother already living away in Hamburg in the first stage of a peripatetic career with women. The new man was a fashionable surgeon with the added distinction of reputed great skill and a professorship at a university. He must have been one of the guests at the dinners and midnight suppers the lively and wealthy widow continued to host after her husband's death. Edgar was a catch, almost a celebrity, his knife restored the health of opera singers and he contributed piquant indiscretions about some of his patients—oh Richard Tauber achieved such sweet high notes because he had only one ball.

Arnulf (but to his mother her son was always 'Arnie') found a kind of elder-brother intimate friend in his mother's substitute husband, if not exactly the substitute father; the biological one had disappeared with childhood and in the adolescent six years since there had formed some sort of scaffolding for the structure of guided adulthood processes missing behind it. Perhaps as fellow male but not one in authority Eddie was an ally in the sociable trio with the flighty mother. There was comfort in unconventional family relations that were unconsciously in line with the shifting of certainties being declaimed by beery oratory in Munich. If that voice was ignored by the new happy couple, the younger son became more and more aware that the professors at his university were preparing him for a life that no longer existed. It would be replaced by the fellow students wearing the swastika instead of sports insignia on their caps who beat him up when he turned for some sort of alternative future by joining the student socialist association. The year he graduated as a Doctor of Philosophy was that of the burning of books. He completed his cycle, so far, to adulthood, by marrying his girl and took authority to urge that the family must leave what had been their native country. Eddie disagreed. They were assimilated, well-connected, no-one would touch them. Arnie was young, leftist therefore misled. A few months later the professor was informed that he was dismissed from his university appointment and in private medical practice could treat only people of his own race, Jews. He shot himself.

EDGAR the surgeon left behind with a bullet in his head. With the Dom Pérignon after the opera, when Richard Tauber sang and Eddie whispered his titillating medical indiscretions to suppressed giggles. In the boardinghouse room her son wanted to rescue her from and that she defended as cosy, she was busy, late nights, writing in the diary the wedding anniversary celebration she was looking forward to, the date with one of her escorts to a musical, the address of a nightclub said to be the place to go, a café date next week with a friend who needed cheering up, her husband just left her for the wife of his golf partner. Incorrigible scatterbrain charming, exasperating in innocent craziness. Her son would shrug, not a serious thought in her dear head; she's always been that way. Her serious son, himself, had spent four years in the Allied army settling their scores with the Nazis.

A grandmother who'd never grown up.

Life: a stack of fancy dress costumes in a pirate chest. No number tattooed on an arm; no. No last journey in a cattle truck.

Who among the responsible adults, grown up at the distance, had found a lover-cum-husband sitting in his consulting room with a revolver bullet in his brain that finally outlawed the doctor-for-Jews-only. Who had put up an umbrella against the Camp de Concentration de Sébikholane as if to shelter from a passing shower.

So what's significant about that?

The past is a foreign country.

No entry.

The past is a foreign country . . .
— L. P. HARTLEY, *The Go-Between*

gregor

ANYONE who is a reader knows that what you have read has influenced your life. By 'reader' I mean one from the time you began to pick out the printed words, for yourself, in the bedtime story. (Another presumption: you became literate in some era before the bedtime story was replaced by the half-hour before the Box.) Adolescence is the crucial period when the poet and the fiction writer intervene in formation of the sense of self in sexual relation to others, suggesting— excitingly, sometimes scarily—that what adult authority has told or implied is the order of such relations, is not all. Back in the Forties, I was given to understand: first, you will meet a man, both will fall in love, and you will marry; there is an order of emotions that goes with this packaged process. That is what love *is*.

For me, who came along first was Marcel Proust. The strange but ineluctable disorder of Charles Swann's agonising love for a woman who wasn't his type (and this really no fault of her own, he fell in love with her as what she was, eh?);

the jealousy of the Narrator tormentedly following a trail of Albertine's evasions.

Swept away was the confetti. I now had different expectations of what experience might have to take on. My apprenticeship to sexual love changed; for life. Like it or not, this is what love *is*. Terrible. Glorious.

But what happens if something from a fiction is not interiorised, but materialises? Takes on independent existence?

It has just happened to me. Every year I re-read some of the books I don't want to die without having read again. This year one of these is Kafka's *Diaries*, and I am about half-way through. It's night-time reading of a wonderfully harrowing sort.

A few mornings ago when I sat down at this typewriter as I do now, not waiting for Lorca's *duende* but getting to work, I saw under the narrow strip of window which displays words electronically as I convey them, a roach. A smallish roach about the size and roach-shape of the nail of my third finger— medium-sized hand. To tell that I couldn't believe it is understatement. But my immediate thought was practical: it was undoubtedly there, how did it get in. I tapped the glass at the place beneath which it appeared. It confirmed its existence, not by moving the body but wavering this way and that two whiskers, antennae so thin and pale I had not discerned them.

I proceeded to lift whatever parts of the machine are accessible, but the strip of narrow glass display was not. I consulted the User's Manual; it did not recognise the eventuality of a cockroach penetrating the sealed refuge meant for words only. I could find no way the thing could have entered, but reasoned that if it had, shiny acorn-brown back, fine-traced antennae, it could leave again at will. Its own or mine. I tapped again overhead on the glass, and now it sidled—which meant, ah, that it was cramped under that roof—to the top limit of the space available. This also revealed bandy black legs like punctuation marks. I called a friend and she reacted simply: It's impossible. Can't be.

Well, it *was*. I have a neighbour, a young architect, whom I see head-down under the bonnet, repairing his car at weekends; there was no course of action but to wait until he could be expected to come home that evening. He is a fixer who can open anything, everything. What to be done in the meantime? Take up where I left off. Send words stringing shadows across the body. Indeed, the disturbance might hope to rouse the intruder somehow to seek the way to leave.

I am accustomed to being alone when I work. I could not help seeing that I was not; something was deliberately *not watching* me—anyway, I couldn't make out its eyes—but was intimately involved with the process by which the imagination finds record, becomes extant.

It was then I received as I hadn't heard in this way before; Can't be.

Night after night I had been reading Franz Kafka's diaries, the subconscious of his fictions, that Max Brod wouldn't destroy. So there it all is, the secret genesis of creation. Kafka's subconscious was nightly conducting me from consciousness to the subconscious of sleep.

Had I *caused* that creature.

Is there another kind of metamorphosis, you don't wake up to find yourself transformed into another species, wriggling on light-brown shiny back and feeling out your space with wispy sensors, but the imagining of such a being can create one, independent of any host, physical genesis; or can imagination summon such a live being to come on out of the woodwork and manifest itself?

What nonsense. There are no doubt the usual domestic pests living clandestinely among and nourished by whatever there is to be nibbled from piles of paper and newspaper cuttings. Who else eats the gilt lettering on book jackets? Next morning he/she/it was still there, no ectoplasm of my imagination, flattened under the glass and moving, with long intervals of watchful immobility, a little way laterally or vertically as the machine warmed in use.

My neighbour had come and studied the situation, or rather Gregor's—I had come to think of the creature that way, never mind. The young architect found that the array of tools he owned were too clumsy for the Italian finesse that had gone into the making of the machine. He would try to borrow a jeweller's tools. Two more days passed and I continued not to be alone as I wrote. At first I wanted the thing in there to die; how could it exist without water, food—and air. As the glass display seemed hermetically sealed, wouldn't any oxygen trapped within be exhausted. Even a beetle, a roach, whatever, must have lungs. Then I began to want it released alive, a miraculous survivor, example of the will to live evidenced beyond its humble size and status in the chain of life. I saw myself receiving it from the deliverer and releasing it on some leaf in the garden. I called the firm from which I had bought the typewriter two years ago to ask for the visit of a know-how mechanic and was told they didn't service obsolete business machines any more, handled only computers.

He, my creature, didn't die; when I would pause a moment to acknowledge him, there under my words, and he was perfectly immobile, I would think, he's gone; that other sense of 'gone', not escaped. Then the remaining antenna would sway, the other had broken off, no doubt in patient efforts to find the secret exit by which he came in. There were times when he hid—I had seen him slip into what must be some sliver of space below where the glass window was flush with its casing. Or I'd glance up: no, not there; and then he'd appear again. My young neighbour had warned, I hope it doesn't lay eggs in there, but I thought of the prisoner as male—maybe just because I'm a woman, assuming the conventional partner I've had in intimate situations faced together. On Friday night I happened to go back into my work-room to fetch a book, turned on the lamp, and there he was, moving up his inch of vertical space and then arrested, frustrated that what he seemed to have forgotten, the way he got in, the way he might get out, was not found. He looked darkened, flat and shiny beetle-black, but that aspect was by lamplight.

Saturday mid-morning my young neighbour arrived with German precision tools arranged like jewellery in a velvet-lined folder. The tenant of the display window was not to be seen; tapping on the glass did not bring him up from his usual hiding-place in that interstice below level of the glass. My neighbour studied more informedly than I had the components of the typewriter as described in Italian, German, French, Japanese and English in the User's Manual and set to work. The machine slowly came apart, resisting with every minute bolt and screw and the rigidity of plastic that threatened to snap. At last, there was the inner chamber, the glass display. It would not yield; the inhabitant did not rise into view despite the disturbance. We halted operations; had he found his egress, got out; then he might be somewhere in the cavern of the machine exposed. No sign. My neighbour was not going to be defeated by the ingenuity of Italian engineer-ing, he tried this tiny implement and that, managing to un-wind the most minute of pin-head screws and disengage complex clamps. With one last thumb-pressure the glass lifted. The shallow cavity beneath, running the width of the machine, was empty. Where was he who had survived there for five days? Had he freed himself and was watching from among papers and newspaper cuttings instead of on a garden leaf. We continued to search the innards of the typewriter. No sign. Then I ran a finger tracing the narrow space where certainly he had been, existed, hadn't he, and felt a change in the surface under my skin. Peered close, and there he was.

His own pyre. Somehow consumed himself.

A pinch of dust. One segment of a black leg, hieroglyph to be decoded.

safety procedures

LORRIE didn't want me to go and was embarrassed to come out with it. My work means that we have lived in different parts of the world and in each there has always been something to be afraid of. Gangsters, extremist political groups Right and Left tossing bombs into restaurants, hijacks, holdups, a city plumb on the line of an earthquake fault. We have long had a compact, with ourselves, with life; life is dangerous. We live with that; in the one certainty that fear is the real killer. We've never gone in for steel grilles on our doors or been afraid to walk in the streets. We've succeeded in keeping our children free; with sensible precautions. But these last few months there have been a number of airline disasters not really accounted for—pilot error, radar control affected by ground staff strikes, possibility of a fellow passenger aboard with the Damocles weapon not overhead but as explosives down in his boot-soles. Who has the ultimate Black Box that really knows. And only a week ago two people shot dead while queuing to register at an airline desk. We usually make love the night before I leave, I kiss the children in the morning and we all accept naturally that we'll talk on the phone the moment I can use my mobile in the terminal of my arrival—with Lorrie, at least, even if it's night for her and day for me. It's as much a routine as going to my executive office of the company every day.

—Why'd you let Isa book you on that route?—

Lorrie knows my secretary organises my schedules with perfect efficiency. —Why not? It's obvious. The best airline to get me where I have to go.—

—But the country it belongs to. In some conflict among them all . . . These days.—

—For God's sake—you know what the security process is like *these days*. Anyway, that airline's country isn't in any hassle between India and Pakistan, Israel and Palestine—whatever. Since when have we given in to fear of flying my darling.— Quoting (if I remember) the title of a book we once read.

—No connection you—we—know of.—

But she's heard what I was really saying: since when do we have a little-wifey boring conventional scene when hubby goes off on business, since when do we cower, you and I, before life as it is.

And then she says something the way she has (part of what I love her for) that strikes aside my patronising inference of little-wifeyness.

—You don't know whose enemy you are.—

—What're you talking about? I'm nobody's enemy.—

—By boarding a plane you become one. There's the line's insignia painted on the tail. Logo of nationality.—

I hugged her quickly in recognition of her special quirky intelligence, and laughed. Our closeness made her smile past the issue. No fuss. That's our way. The company driver picked me up and delivered me to the airport.

Good young Isa had reserved my favourite seat, window, not too far back in the business class cabin (the company has decided to be globally politically correct, no more first class wasteful expenditure), but not near the toilets and galley—too many people queuing up to pee and too much chatter among the attendants.

There was a long flight ahead with time sliding backwards all the way. On these journeys I keep home time, I don't change my watch until I reach time as measured at my destination. Wonder how many hours of my life-span I've lost— maybe gained?—on these many trips to and fro across date-lines.

I tell people I actually like to work in planes, I can take out my laptop and prepare myself for the meetings and decisions awaiting me, in productive isolation among strangers. It's not often there's someone I know on the same flight, and if there should be I don't want any change of seat to place me beside an acquaintance. Of course, in recent years there's been the unavoidable distraction of the fold-out individual TV screen which goes with every seat, and invariably my anonymous neighbour will have the thing set up and flickering away in my peripheral vision although thank God the sound passes directly into the individual's ears, spares mine. The truth is—no, the fact is—truth's too important a word for such a trivially boastful lie—it's never long before I pack away the monitor of my industriousness, the laptop, wrestle a few minutes with folding back the pages of the newspapers offered (why aren't there special tabloid editions of *The New York Times*, *Herald Tribune*, *Figaro*, *Frankfurter Allgemeine*, *Corriere della Sera*, et al.,

for airline distribution) and then look—gaze—at what's outside. The window: nothing. All right. The void that, from the
ground, is called the sky. Intruded by puffy herds and castles
of cloud for a while, scribbled across with a fading vapour
trail, a chalked rainbow drawn by another plane out of sight.
Other times become an enclosing grey-white element without
latitude or longitude or substance like blindness descended
upon the eyes. Perhaps what I'm saying is that I've half dozed-
off, there's an inbetween form of consciousness that's not experienced anywhere else but up here. With nothing. The cosy
cockpit voice keeps exhorting its charges to sit back and relax.
But this state is not relaxation, it's another form of being I
have for a while and have never told anyone about, even Lorrie
(specially, perhaps, not Lorrie, with marriage it's possible you
give too much about yourself away).

Nothing. Up there, out there, I do not have within me
love, sex, wife, children, house and executive office. I do not
have a waiting foreign city with international principals and
decisions. Why has no artist—not even the abstractionists—
painted this state attainable only since the invention of passenger aircraft? The gaze. Freedom.

On this trip I have beside me—I notice only when the bar
trolley pauses at my row—a middle-aged woman who's evidently slim, doesn't overflow or hog the armrest space between
us, something at least in her favour. We exchange 'Good
evening' and that's that. She is good-looking (as her face turns
towards me in the brief greeting) in an impersonal way, without any projection of her fiftyish remains of beauty, as if the
face is something she has assumed as you take along an umbrella. I dread, on my numerous long flights, someone in the
next seat who wants to talk and will take up a monologue if

you don't respond. This one, apparently, no more wanted conversation than I did. She didn't set up her TV screen, either. I was aware that after dinner was served she leant forward and took from her cabin bag a book.

I suppose it was the food, the wine. I returned to the laptop, to the presence within me of the voice and body of my wife, the hands of my children upon me, the boardroom, known expressions of the faces, and the issues I was to meet. Nothing. Replaced by tomorrow.

As I worked at my computer and time was lost in passage the aircraft began to shudder. The seatbelt sign was illuminated. Turbulence, we expect to climb out of it, the cockpit voice soothingly reassured. But my window went black—it was afternoon, not nightfall—the swollen black of a great forest of storm. Out of nothing: this was the other power, like the opposition of Evil to Good religions tell us about on earth. I was determined to ignore what became the swooping, staggering of the plane, its teeth-chattering of overhead lockers, the collision of trolleys, spilling of glasses. I tried to focus on the screen of the laptop jiggling on my knees, but my eyes refused to function. As I managed to stow the laptop in a seat pocket I saw the woman beside me had put down her book. In a violent lurch of the enraged structure that encased us the book flung itself from her lap to the floor. I watched it slither onto the aisle, where it was joined by someone's shoes taken off, as we do on long flights, for comfort. Now the cockpit voice commanded everyone to stay seated, forbidden to walk about the cabin, make sure your seatbelt is securely fastened. *For your own safety.*

I've weathered (that old cliché) a few spells of 'turbulence' in the hundreds of flights I've survived. There was never in my memory anything like this. Lorrie feared for me: a hijack. This was a hijack by the elements. Whatever force had us wouldn't let go, no escape by gaining height or lowering it. There were crashes sounding from the galley. Two cabin attendants collided and the one fell across a passenger's head. The commands from the cockpit became a gabble. Behind the seats where the woman and I were strapped, trapped, someone was vomiting in heaving waves and gurglings. The plane dropped as under a great blow and then bounced this side and that. It wanted to rid itself of us, our laptops, our headsets, our dutyfree, the caverns weighed with bags of possessions we lug around the world as if our life depends upon them.

Our life.

The voice from the cockpit made itself heard through broken-up amplification, the captain was going to attempt an emergency landing at a military airfield whose name I recognised as a sign that we had been blown off course. A woman was screaming, there were sobs and voices calling out for help—from whom, where?—praying—to whom, for what? My heart thudded wildly Lorrie's fear: now mine. I suddenly realised that while everyone was appealing in the solidarity of human terror to everyone else, the woman beside me and I had not looked to each other, had not spoken. So I turned to her.

Incredible.

She was sitting calmly with one hand loose upon the other, not clutching—the seat the armrests anything—as I was. She was letting the fury of the plane slap her about, her lips at rest, no grimace of the animal fear that was everyone's face. She flicked her quiet open eyes to acknowledge my presence, this unknown human who was going to die in intimacy beside me. My last woman. And then she turned directly to me and I heard again the voice that had spoken only once, two words, Good evening.

—It's all right. The plane will somehow land. You're safe. Everyone.—

I didn't know if she was unbelievably courageous, duped by some religious faith, or mad.

She spoke again, her head resisting the tumultuous pulls against her body. —It won't happen. Because I'm aboard. This last year I have to tell you I have tried three times, three different ways, to end my life. Failed. No way out for me. So it seems I can't die, no flight I take will kill.—

T H E order came from the cockpit to assume the emergency landing position, heads bowed over knees. The plane struck the earth as if it would crack the rock of the world. We descended in a fairly orderly way—those desperate to live pushing through women-and-children-first, I restraining the instinct—by slides let down from the plane's sides. Banners of flame unfurled about it behind us as we ran. In the confusion I did not see whether the woman was among us, the saved, all of us.

I'm sure she was.

mother tongue

BUT everything's by chance—how else would she ever have met him? Been here.

THEY fell in love in her country. Met there.

A taxi he had taken skidded into her small car. It was raining the way Europe weeps in winter, and the taxi driver slammed out of his vehicle and accosted her from the other side of her window, streaming water as if dissolving in anger. His passenger intervened, exonerating her and citing the weather as responsible. The damage to taxi and car was minimal; names, addresses and telephone numbers were exchanged for the purpose of insurance claims. —A hoo-hah about nothing.— He said that to her as if this was something he and she, in their class as taxi patron and private car owner would rate it before the level of indignation of the Pakistani or whatever the taxi man was. The passenger spoke in English, native to him, but saw through the blur of rain the uncertain nod of one who has heard but not quite understood. He didn't know a colloquial turn of phrase to translate the passing derision into that country's language.

How he came to call her had to do with a document he was to sign, as witness; couldn't have been an opportunity to follow up any attraction to a pretty face, because the rain had made hers appear smeary as the image in a tarnished mirror. So they met again, over a piece of paper in a café near the lawyer's office where she worked. It was of course still raining, and he was able to make conversation with his cobbled-together vocabulary in the country's language, remarking that you didn't have days on end like this where he came from; that's how she learnt: from Africa. *South Africa. Mandela.* The synapses and neurons made the identifying connection in the map of every European mind. Yes, he had picked up something of her language, although the course he'd taken in preparation hadn't proved of much use when he arrived and found himself where everybody spoke it all the time and not in phrase-book style and accent. They laughed together at the way *he* spoke it, a mutual recognition closer, with the flesh-and-bone structure, shining fresh skin, deep-set but frank eyes, before him in place of the image in the tarnished mirror. Blond hair—real blond, he could tell from experience of his predilection for Nordic types, genuine or chemically concocted (once naked, anyway, they carelessly showed their natural category). She knew little of his language, the few words she remembered, learnt at school. But the other forms of recognition were making communication between them. They began to see each other every day; she would take his calls on her mobile, carried into the corridor or the women's room out of earshot of others in the lawyer's office. There among the wash-basins and toilet booths the rendezvous was decided.

He worked for one of the vast-tentacled international advertising agencies, and had got himself sent to her country by yet another kind of recognition; the director's, of his intelligence, adaptability, and sanguine acceptance of the need to learn the language of the country to which he would be sent as one of the co-ordinators of the agency's conglomerate hype (global, they called it). He was not a copywriter or designer, he was a businessman who, as he told her, had many friends and contacts of his generation in different enterprises and might— as they were all on the lookout for—move on to some other participation in the opportunities of their world. By this he also meant his and hers, both of them young. He saw that world of theirs, though they were personally far apart geographically, turning round technology as the earth revolves round the sun.

She shared an apartment with a girl-friend; the first love-making was in his apartment where he lived, alone, since coming to Germany some months past. He had had his share of affairs at home—that surely must be, in view of his composed, confidently attractive face, the lean sexual exuberance of his body, and his quick mind; by lapse of e-mails and calls between them, the affair with someone back there was outworn. The girl met by chance probably had had a few experiments. She spoke of 'a boy-friend' who had emigrated somewhere. Of course she might just be discreet and once they were in their sumptuous throes of love-making, what went before didn't matter. Her flesh was not abundant but alertly responsive— a surprising find. He'd thought of German female types as either rather hefty, athletic, or fat.

But it was her tenderness to him, the loving*ness* in the sexuality that made this foreign affair somewhat different from the others, so that—he supposed it's what's called falling in love—they married. In love. Passed that test. An odd move in his life, far from what would have been expected, among his circle at home. But powerful European countries are accustomed to all sorts of invasions, both belligerent and peaceful, and this foreign one was legal, representing big business, an individual proof of the world's acceptance of Germany's contrition over the past. He was suitably well received when she took him to her family, and as a welcome novelty among her friends. With their easy company he became more fluent in the to-and-fro of their language. And of course it was the language of the love affair and the marriage that had been celebrated in true German style, a traditional festivity which her circle of friends, who had moved on to an unceremonious lifestyle, nevertheless delightedly animated around the veiled bride and three-piece-suited groom. His was a personality and a growing adeptness in exchanges that, in their remaining months there, made Germany a sort of his-and-hers.

She knew when she began to love this man that the condition would be that she would live in another country. A country she had never seen, touched the earth, felt the wind or sun, rain, heard in its expression by its inhabitants, except through him, touch of his skin, sound of his voice; a country landscaped by his words. Love goes wherever the beloved must. The prospect of going home with him to Africa: her friends saw that she was—first time since they'd all grown up together—exalted. The anticipation actually showed in the burnish of the shine over her fine cheekbones and the eagerness in her readied eyes. She ceased to see the Bauhaus façade of the building where the lawyer's offices were, the familiar tower of the ancient church that had survived the bombs of the parents' war, the beer *stube* where she was among those friends. Her parents: how did that church's marriage ceremony put it? An old biblical injunction along with many of the good precepts she had learnt at the Lutheran Sunday school they had sent her to as a child. 'Leave thy father and thy mother and cleave only . . .' Something like that. The emotional parting with the parents, handed from the arms of one to the other, each jealous to have the last embrace of the daughter, was not a parting but an arrival in the embrace of a beloved man.

THEY were in Africa. His Africa, now defined out of a continent. Further defined: his city there. The property market, he was told by his friends who wanted to bring him up-to-date with what was happening while he was away 'doing the disappearing act into the married man', was 'flat on its arse' and this was the time to do what married men did, quit the bachelor pad and buy a house. So they spent only a month in his apartment that was to her a hotel room vacated by a previous occupant. She didn't know any of the objects in it which must have been personal to the man she had not known while he lived there. She looked through his books, took down one here and there as if she were in a library expecting to find some particular subject, but even when he was absent did not touch letters she saw lying in a drawer she had pulled out to find a ballpoint likely to be at hand in the unit of desk, computer, fax and photocopier. When they bought a house and he decided the only furniture worth taking along was the complex of his communications outfit, he cleared into a garbage bin the bundle of letters along with other papers, outlived.

The house new to them was in fact an old house, as age is measured in a city founded as a gold-mining camp 120 years ago. His white parents' generation were all for steel and glass or fake Californian-Spanish, didn't want to live with wooden verandah rails and coal-burning fire-places. To their offspring generation the Frank Lloyd Wright and Hispano-Californian look-alikes were symbolic of people looking to take on an identity outside the one they weren't sure of. Even if they didn't think in this way of their impulse to be worldly-fashionable, the assumed shell was also another shelter in their chosen isolation from the places, the manner in which the black people who surrounded, outnumbered them, lived: in hovels and shacks. Young whites on an economic level of choice found the old high-ceilinged, corrugated-iron-roofed houses more interestingly built, spacious for adaptation to ways of a life open to the unexpected. Everyone was doing it; fixing up old places. Blacks too, the professionals, media people and civil servants in what was called the new dispensation—civic term for what used to be called freedom. The houses were short of bathrooms, but those were easily installed, just as the kitchen, in the house he bought, was at once renovated with the equipment she knew—as the model of her mother's in Germany—was essential.

Home. A real his-and-hers. Friends came to help him thin overgrown trees, she had the beer chilled and the snacks ready for this male camaraderie. She planted flowers she had never seen before, didn't bloom where she came from. She hadn't found work yet—that wasn't urgent, anyway, her share in the creation of the house was a new and fulfilling occupation, as anything in the service of devotion is, centred by the big bed where they made love. There was the suggestion that she might find part-time employment to interest her at the local Goethe Institute. But she didn't want to be speaking German—English was her language now. She was introduced to, plunged into immersion in his circle. She talked little, although back in her own country, her circle where he'd made a place for himself so easily, she was rather animated. Here, she listened; it seemed to be her place. She was happy to feel she was understanding everything said in his language, even if she couldn't use it confidently enough to speak up.

There were many parties. Even without any special occasion, his friends black and white clustered instinctively in this or that apartment, house or bar, like agents of some cross-pollination of lives.

On a terrace the sunken sun sends pale searchlights to touch a valance of clouds here and there, the darkness seems to rise from damp grass as the drinking ignites animation in his friends. She has asked him to stop the car on the way, where there's a flower-seller on a corner. —What for? No-one's birthday, far as I know.— He forgets it's the rule, in her country, to take flowers or chocolates—some gift—to a party. —Wine'd have been a better idea, my sweet.— And it happens that the host or one of the hosts—it's a combined get-together— dumps the bunch of lilies on a table where they are soon pushed aside by glasses and ashtrays.

When they arrived she sat beside him. At these gatherings married people don't sit together, it's not what one does, bringing a cosy domesticity into a good-time atmosphere. But she's still a newcomer, innocent of the protocol and he's too fond to tell her she should—well, circulate. She's one of the prettiest women there: looks fresh-picked; while the flowers she brought wilt. She's younger than most of the women. She sits, with the contradiction of knees and feet primly aligned and the lovely foothills of breasts showing above the neckline of her gauzy dress. Perhaps the difference between her and the others is she's prepared herself to look her best to honour him, not to attract other men.

He gets up to go over and greet someone he thinks has forgotten him—he's been away in Europe a whole year—and when the shoulder-grasping embrace, the huge laughter, is over, comes back, but by chance in the meantime someone has been waved to the seat next to his wife. So he pulls up a chair on the woman's other side. He hasn't deserted—it's a threesome. His newly-imported wife happens to have already met this woman on some other occasion within the circle. The woman is very attractive, not really young anymore but still wild, riling the company with barbed remarks, running hands up through her red-streaked plumage as if in a switch to despair at herself. People are distracted from their own talk by her spectacle. More wine is tilted into glasses as they come up to laugh, interject. The husband is one of her butts. He's challenging a reminiscence of an incident in the friends' circle his neighbour is recounting, flourishing loudly. All around the wife are references back and forth, a personal lingo—every clique has this, out of common experience. It was the same, among her friends in that past life in Germany. Jokes you don't understand even if you know the words; understand only if you're aware what, who's being sent up. She doesn't know, either, the affectionate, patronising words, phrases, that are the means of expression of people who adapt and mix languages, exclamations, word-combinations in some sort of English that isn't the usage of educated people like themselves. There are so many languages in this country of theirs that his friends don't speak, but find it amusing to bring the flavours of into their own with the odd word or expression; so much more earthy, claiming an identity with their country as it is, now. Anecdotes are being argued—interruptions flying back and forth as voices amplify over re-filled glasses.

. . . so *they threw him with a stone*, right?—the director's office, *nogal* . . .

. . . *In your face*. That's her always . . . *Hai! Hamba kahle* . . .

. . . *Awesome!* Something to do with a sports event or, once, a dessert someone made? They use the word often in talk of many different kinds; she's looked it up in a dictionary but there it means 'inspiring awe, an emotion of mingled reverence, dread and wonder'. And there are forms of address within the circle borrowed from other groups, other situations and experiences they now share. Someone calls out—*Chief*, I want to ask you something—when neither the speaker nor the pal hailed, white or black (for the party is mixed) is tribal—as she knows the title to be, whether in Indonesia, Central America, Africa, anywhere she could think of. Some address one another as *My China*. How is she to know this is some comradely endearment, cockney rhyming slang—'my mate, my china plate'—somehow appropriated during the days of apartheid's army camps.

Smiling, silent; to be there with him is enough.

The party becomes a contest between him and the woman who sits between them. Each remembers, insists on a different version of what the incident was.

—You're confounding it with that time everyone was shagging in the bushes!—

—Well, you would be reliable about *that*—

—Listen, listen, listen to me!— He slaps his arm round the back of her neck, under the hair she's flung up, laughing emphasis. She puts a hand on his thigh: —*You* never listen—

It's a wrestling match of words that come from the past, with touch that comes from the past. The hand stays on him. Then he snatches it up palm to palm, shaking it to contradict what she's jeering, laughing close to his face and drowning out the calls of others. —O-O-O you were still in *kort broek*, My China! Loverboy—you remember Isabella that time water skiing? Kama Sutra warns against games under water—

—No ways! You're the one to talk—also did some deep-diving in search of marine life, *ek sê*. No-oo, *kahle-kahle* was my line!—

—And what happened to your great fancy from where was it, Finland. That Easter. Well why not—whatever you did's politically correct with me, they say the grave's a fine and private place but no *okes* do there embrace— Among the well-read of the friends this adaptation of Marvell was uproariously appreciated.

She was alone and laughed—she did not know what at. She sat beside the woman and her husband who were hugging, celebrating each other in the easy way of those who have old connections of intimacy encoded in exchanges of a mother tongue, released by wine and a good time had by all. She laughed when everyone else did. And then sat quiet and nobody noticed her. She understood she didn't know the language.

The only mother tongue she had was his in her mouth, at night.

allesverloren

WHOM to talk to.

Grief is boring after a while, burdensome even to close confidants. After a very short while, for them.

The long while continues. A cord that won't come full circle, doesn't know how to tie a knot in resolution. So whom to talk to. Speak.

It comes down to the impossible, the ridiculous: talk then; about *this*! But to whom. Nobody knew about it. No, of course there must be some friends among those who surrounded us all those years of ours who did know, but since it was not spoken by them, it didn't ever happen.

So whom to talk to. Necessary; to bring him back, piece him together, his life that must continue to exist for his survivor. Talk to.

There's no-one.

Wind shivers along blue plastic covering the pergola of the house next door.

Wind in sun over the sea; come, abandon that crazy component of the quest and travel to contemplate an ocean!

Wind wags the trees' heads. No message there, for the survivor.

Nothing to avoid it. There's only one.

To supply answers to questions that were never asked, never necessary to be asked in an intimacy of flesh and mind that reassured, encompassed and transfigured everything, all pasts, into the living present? Answers. Is that what such *understanding*, coming to terms with loss, will prove to be? For so far understanding has turned out to have no meaning. *Come to lunch, come to the theatre, attend the meeting, take up new interests, there's your work, you're a historian—for Christ' sake, it's important.* Grief is speaking a language that reaches no-one's ears, drawing hieroglyphs for which there is no cracked code. 'Nor hope nor dread attend the dying animal / Man has created death.' Everyone fears death but no-one admits to the fear of grief; the revulsion at that presence, there in us all.

Thinking about it (about the One) and not acting. The trivial irritabilities that are the only distraction; e.g., no bananas left today in the fruit bowl—regression to the quick fix of a child's craving to eat something it likes best.

SHE, the survivor, was divorced when she met the man who was to be hers, and so was he, her man who now is dead— months ago, the long while beyond the short while when others still talked of him with her. She had had a couple of brief affairs in the interim between divorce and the marriage, and he had had only one. That was not the difference. It was with

a man. He had told her of it as part of the confidentiality, con-
fessions, that come as the relief of another kind of blessed
orgasm after the first few of love-making. A form of deep grat-
itude that is going to be part of love for the other being, if
there is going to be love.

There was love and there is love, but only on one side; the
reciprocal recipient is gone. Gone? That implies somewhere.
There is no somewhere in this death that man has invented.
Because if the poet is right, man invented it, there's no
Divine-supplied invention of an after-life in a fully-furnished
heaven or torture-equipped hell gymnasium. The beloved
hasn't gone anywhere. He is dead. He is nowhere except in the
possibility of recall, a calling-up of all the times, phases,
places, emotions and actions of what he was, how he lived
while he *was*. Almost half that life—you don't count childhood, of course—was theirs. What came before was thought
of by them as a sort of prolonged adolescence—full of the
mistakes and misconceptions of that state: the two early marriages, his and hers, rather inconceivable, in the knowledge of
this one, theirs. The one and only, he would say to her, the
days he was dying. The conclusion along with his own coming
conclusion.

He had had no children in that first marriage and they had
no idea where she, the woman, was—gone to South America,
when last her name came up somehow. Unlikely by example of
his earthy experience of mayhem with her, that she was still
with the man who'd taken her to Peru or wherever. It was
agreed between the two who had found the treasure of each
other that they had been both naïve and culpable—no excuses—in those marriage episodes; maybe these had even been

an initiation for their own: an experience of everything a mating should not be, so that they would be freed to make a real one, theirs.

So she knew, from her experience doubling with his, what emotions, illusions and disillusions, impulsive responses, compromises (how could any intelligent person have been deceived by such obvious contradictions) could bring about so-called marriages. The woman was a Beauty, and the classic case of the disturbed childhood never left behind, taking revenge on the world through the man who had chosen her; her chance of savage rejection. He had tried to make something of what was the hopelessness of the marriage, refused to recognise this, tried to persuade the woman to go with him to psychiatrists and psychotherapists, marriage counsellors, and when she cursed and jeered at him, went alone to lie on the couch.

In their emotional blunders, what she (is it possible she now has the archaic category Widow, out of the range of Miss, Mrs, Ms) had not experienced as he had, was his affair with one of his own sex. How it came about she could and had fully entered with him; the 'unnaturalness' of it—not in the sense of some moral judgment on homosexuals, but that she knew, in the exalted gratification he found in her femaleness, that *this* was what was natural to *his* sexuality. It had happened as part of the ugly desperation and humiliation of the first marriage. He would accept any distraction, then. Any invitation to attend gatherings and conferences anywhere. Get away. At an architectural conference he was lined up in the inevitable group photograph; found himself at breakfast next day taking the only free seat, at a table with the photographer. Then talking to him again when encountered in the evening at the hotel pool. The photographer was virtually the only person he had any real exchange with in three days; he himself made no contribution to discussions, he heard but did not follow his architect and town-planner colleagues' discourses, he was cut off in parched despair of his failure to create some bearable relationship with the woman who was supposed to be his wife; and filled with self-disgust at his failure. The photographer—well, of course—had an unexpected lens on life. An interesting man. He saw wars and floods, nature's disasters, the features of strikers and politicians, not a Fury whose image blocked all else. The two men were the same age in years, but not in their conception of themselves. The photographer offered in place of emasculating catastrophic rejection a simple acceptance of something never imagined, unthinkable in relation to oneself as a man: her man. In that state, she supposed, you could have been grateful for any recognition, any tenderness from a fellow human being: something hardly believed possible could happen.

I'm not bisexual, he had told her long ago, in the confessionals of their beginning. It has been the only time ever. It was some months but to me it's the blank you had a day when you were young and had been drunk all night, your friends told you.

Now that she has seen him dead, felt him cold, she finds there's something *she* can't quite remember—what does it matter—whether he divorced before or after that lapse that was like the blankout of alcohol. Must have told her which, but told nothing else, was asked nothing else by her. No more than he would have put any value on hearing details of her love affairs—and her marriage, unlike his, had no traumatic drama to recount, was amicably ended through mutual agreement that each was leaving youth by differing signposts, shouldn't foolishly have set out on zigzag footsteps.

But now that her man can exist for her survival only through piecing him together in what is available for recall, there is a gap—yes, a blankout. She can make the re-creation for herself whole only if she can recall what is not hers to recall.

Whom to talk to. There's only one. One who can recall.

IF nobody knows or cares where the Beauty has gone to grow old the one who was the photographer has not disappeared. As if her eye, now, were programmed to react to the small print of the name appearing in accreditation to a series of newsprint photographs, there it is, Hayford Leiden. She had been told this name in the lovers' confessional, long ago. Over the years the modest byline must have appeared here and there in the local and international newspapers she and her man read, but who notices the minute print below the picture?

She wrote in the dark of her head a letter that never got to paper, addressed care of a photographic agency called Magnum whose name often appeared in attributions in place of that of an individual photographer. Where did he live? If she received his address, what would the unwritten letter convey to him? Would he know that the man of the affair, her man, was dead. Probably not, since their circles had not overlapped in all the years of the marriage. She taught history at a university and knew how the alternative history of private lives goes unnoticed by those concentrated on public events; and a news photographer is one such. So the letter was there, as if waiting to be printed out, so to speak, from a word-processor.

She thought of travelling—friends prescribed it—to move away for a time from the environment of her grief, and perhaps to remove her from their necessity to contemplate it. She, in her turn, could accept invitations to conferences as a substitute way of life as her man once had resorted to. There was one from Canada she passed over, but she overcame her reluctance to leave the rooms, the house where his presence was still recognised by his hairbrush in the bathroom and the grubby chairarms where his hands had rested, and accepted the invitation to a conference in an English university city, which perhaps would seem to be less interesting. She didn't know whether this was so; and whether she had made the choice because the byline of the photographer whose name she was aware of appeared in newspapers from England that she read. She might visit some friends in England although she had not told any of them she was coming. To pass the time while waiting for the call to board her flight she wandered around the dutyfree shop and passing the wine section saw a red wine she and her man had particularly liked, picked up a bottle. Friends might enjoy it as a reminiscent taste of the home in Africa they had left behind.

Once in the provincial English city, an intention came clear to her: she called various photographic agencies in London and was given his address and telephone number. So the voyage admitted its purpose. She stepped back from herself: in half-disapproval. The letter never was written but the telephone call was made. The first time there was a reprieve; an answering service at which she left no message. The next time a man said yes, Hayford Leiden speaking. She gave her name, so-and-so's wife, in a calm, friendly voice, might have been a caller about to make a sales-pitch. Could she come and see him, briefly. His surprise (or lack of comprehension—what does this woman want) was well disguised; he was no doubt accustomed, in his work, to bizarre encounters. Totally tied up for the coming week, but if she cared to come to London, say, the following Friday . . . yes, he remembers her man, met him some years ago.

He is dead, she said. Not long ago. Oh, he was sorry to hear . . . She would like to talk; nothing personal, she assured, just some dates, events, places, his architectural activities in a period of her man's career when she had not known him. *Nothing personal.*

The meeting, appointment—whatever—she was still at odds with herself over its presumption, thrusting her life upon a stranger—was for the afternoon. Fiveish, he had suggested. She decided she would stay the night in London at a hotel, inventing some excuse for missing the evening event at the conference.

O N the train she was inwardly shaking her head over herself; what was she about. She had some rhetorical suspicions. Is there prurience somewhere sneaking hidden in the woman making this visit. Oh why wound herself with such an accusation. She had emphasised it over the phone: nothing personal. Intimacies left understood; those had nothing to do with her, nothing to do with her man when he entered her and she took him. Nothing personal. Certainly the photographer accepted that, or he would not have agreed to the meeting.

When the taxi from Waterloo delivered her to the address—she did not think it would have been this, a majestic Victorian house advanced to the present with extensions of a sun-room, an adjoining roof-terraced flat, and as she took the path to the main portico, the glimpse past the house walls of a green sweep of garden and trees. The word 'Crescent' on her piece of paper had meant to her a semi-circle of dreary London terrace houses sharing identical façades and joined in a single common unit. This house turned its back on the street and apparently shared nothing but access to a large round park exclusive to itself and its circle of neighbours. Could a photographer afford such a place; he must be famous—but what would she know about the economics of the publicity professions. A tile inset on the entry wall flourished the names:

HAYFORD LEIDEN
CHARLES DEVENMORE

She heard his footsteps coming to her before the door opened.

There had been no photograph of him to go by: thick white hair and thick black eyebrows, bold as in a Japanese print. A man who had aged well smiling on what were still his own teeth. The face was smoothly dull-tanned (acquired under a sun-lamp in a male beauty salon no doubt). But no, the back of the hand that came out to greet hers was darker. He wasn't tinted by African bloodline, which she would always recognise, but by some other, Oriental. Still handsome as he once must have been beautiful.

The voice was careless and pleasant, as if to convey, I am ready for you, I know who you are, we know who we are, vis-à-vis one another.

As they sat in Corbusier-design chairs regarded by masks from some Eastern culture and West African ones she knew familiarly, there was small talk about what she was doing in England—holiday assumed.

She was at a conference. Her line (his phrase)? Historian. Ah. That seemed to allow this visit an acceptable context for both these strangers, let them off the hook of whatever linked them. Some aspect of her professional inclination. That would do. The dates, places, of an individual life which go to make up what Tolstoy defined as the collective life of the aggregate of human beings. —I met Marc at a conference, used to do some lined-up group photography in those days, as well as what I really wanted—don't remember what that particular talkshop was all about.—

—You wouldn't have an old diary with the title of the conference? He must have mentioned it but there's no note among his papers, and I didn't pay attention . . .—

A kindly smile quickly became a dismissive turn-down of the lips, keeping his distance. —My god, no, there were so many I could say bye-bye to and see the world instead.—

She understood he was telling her, if she somehow didn't know, that he was a news photographer of repute who had himself, far and wide, contributed images to history.

—Marc stayed on a while after the conference. In this country. Can you tell me where he lived? In London. I'd like to see the house, or the street.—

For a moment he was arranging his reply. —I think some small hotel in Kensington.—

He gauged her.

—My flat was in Notting Hill. He moved in. Some months.—

—What was he doing. Work, I mean. With a firm of architects. Or . . . ? He was someone who was always caught up in his projects.— Her hands opened slowly on the space of his death.

—Oh he was recovering from that mess in his life, we had some good times, he got on famously with my crowd then—all gone our particular ways now. USA, Australia, Spain—South Africa.— This last reference apparently reminded him that this one of the crowd, he had just been told, was dead. —Oh good times, there was the project we did together with an artist friend of mine—I think it might even be around still today, second-hand in some museum somewhere—it was a kind of demountable 'environment'—very ahead of our generation—that's what we called it, he did the architectural shell, the artist did some sort of *objets trouvés* interior stuff, I did the photographs, it was supposed to represent the essential mishmash of our style of living at the time. I think some institute in Manchester—imagine, of all places—commissioned it and it was exhibited here in London, too. Hardly made waves, but we were wild about it together.—

—I thought he took a special refresher course at an architectural institute for a few weeks. Oxford.—

—Not that I know of. He was here in London. Maybe it was something . . . Yes, there was the idea we'd also do a book together, I'd photograph buildings and he'd write the text on their—what'd he call it—architectural relation to the politics of their period. I even had a publisher friend who pretended to be interested . . . The bits of text, maybe even the designs for the 'environment' thing must have lain around in that little flat until I cleared an accumulation of all sorts of stuff when I moved to one of the others I lived in before—here. Finally. He didn't bring anything like that back with him?—

—Not among the papers I've found. It would have been interesting as part of his vision as an architect I'm hoping to put together; there're all the conventional plans that he designed in his practice. I have those.—

Her host became hostly, or backed away from the rising past he had summoned. —Wouldn't you like a drink? Or tea, coffee? Whisky? Vodka?—

—Thank you. If you are having one—vodka, please, with tonic.—

An antique butler's tray table was crowded with liquor bottles and glasses. He left her to fetch ice and tonic water; in the brief absence she could take the chance to look round at what the room held—but they could not be relevant, these Lucian Freud and Bacon nudes, these photographs of the host and another man (Charles Devenmore?) enlaced on a beach, or each individually, one behind his camera in a ruined city, the other on a stage, Shakespearean open-mouthed with rage (the lover evidently an actor)—these could not have been the objects her man had lived this other life among; in that small shared flat, too long ago.

He prepared the drinks and when he had given her hers lifted his own in the social ease therefore supposed between them—a moment in which he might have been going to toast—the past: her man, his man—quickly dismissed so that she might not notice. But she had; the moment lay between them to be examined. He approached it in a generalised way, side-lining what she had said on the telephone. *Nothing personal.* Only dates, places, professional activities in those months in the shared flat, to bring her man back, piece him together, his life that must continue to exist for her survival.

—It's always a problem to get people—other people—to

understand the kind of commune of gays. What someone from outside can find in it that I don't think—I know—doesn't function among the other groups. Something to do with a minority, the healing to be found with us—I don't mean some solemn holy-male thing . . .—

She stirred denial, in her chair. —We've had—I have many good friends among homosexuals . . .—

He took an audible gulp of his vodka and laughed, with a gesture to her to do the same. —Oh yes some of my best friends are Jews man's best friend is his dog.—

What could she say? She was not equipped for this kind of repartee, it was not the encounter or the occasion for it, if he was choosing to make her the butt of insults he'd received in his lifetime. She had told, told him, *nothing personal* and now he was transgressing the limits of recall she had assured him of.

He was suddenly looking at her in an inescapable way she couldn't elude, couldn't interpret, confidential or goading.

—Of course I didn't want him to go.—

Why did this man who had forgotten her man among many others, couldn't give her the plain facts that were all she asked of him, want to assert—claim shared feelings with her: her man who had left her for death, his sometime lover who had left him; their man. Was it amusing him to do so? He went on to recount as an old incident recalled for her benefit—I'd gone off on a trip with someone else, it was to Surinam. As you can see, I'm half-and-half, the name Dutch, the skin Malay, fine old colonial ancestry, isn't it. I had a notion to find my Malay roots there, the new affair went along with this. *He* didn't understand it was an adventure I needed at the time.

So when I returned to our flat I found the place empty—he'd gone back to South Africa. I don't know to what. That crazy woman. God knows.—

—If he wasn't divorced before you met him he divorced then.— She knew herself being lured into confidences never meant to come about.

He poured himself another vodka, gestured to her glass, over which she placed her palm. —I'll tell you something. I did come to South Africa once, maybe ten, twelve years ago. On an assignment. I asked whether he was around; so then I heard about you. Just curious, what had become of him. Some-one told me where you and he lived. But I didn't try to look him up, considering . . .—

There was a hiatus that could not be called silence because while they did not speak there was passing between them a vivid dialogue of the unexpressed.

Then she took up the ready lug of ordinary social inter-course, slotted into place the polite visitor about to leave. —Well, thank you for letting me bother you, I must be off, now.—

—Sure you won't have another drink?—

She was standing, ready for the lie, also. —My train to catch.—

As she hung her bag over her shoulder some hard shape in it nudged her hip; she had forgotten to give the man the bot-tle of wine she had brought along at the last minute before closing the door of her conference hotel room—as she knew she wasn't going to look up the friends she had bought it for, it had seemed to serve as a useful gesture of apology for an intrusion.

He received it with appreciative pleasure. —All the way

from South Africa! Charlie and I'll regale ourselves tonight.—
He read out the name on the label, two words run into
one, most likely those of a Boer wine farmer after the old war
lost to the British, the defeated still spelling in Dutch from
which his own language, Afrikaans, derived. —*Allesverloren*,
'everything lost'—ah, you see, from my Holland side—
grandmother—I can translate . . .—

She walked block after block before remembering to look
for a taxi or bus stop. Should have asked if there was perhaps a
photograph from that time. Could have, since the terms of the
visit had been violated. But no.

You know the one you knew. Cannot know the other, any
other. Allesverloren.

history

THE parrot's been thirty years an attraction in this restaurant, but of course nobody knows how old it is. A parrot can live for a century, it's said—probably an old seafarer's tale; didn't the birds used to be sailors' companions on ancient lonely voyages? They were brought to Europe from Africa, the Amazon, everywhere what was thought of as The World sent ships lurching, venturing the seas to worlds known by others. Those others couldn't speak, so far as the sailors were concerned—that is, not the language of the sailors, whatever it might be. But the bird could. Very soon it asked questions, made demands, cursed, even laughed in their language. The world of others talked back from what The World was set to make of those others—its own image. The sailors didn't know—does anyone—how a bird can speak. But it did. And as if it understood, at least the laughter, the abuse. Else how could it have produced the expression of these?

That's all centuries ago, the restaurant parrot must have come from a pet shop, although Madame Delancy remembers it was given to her husband by some friend. —We would never have bought a parrot! For a restaurant! It's not a zoo!— But she gives a tilt-of-the-head greeting to the parrot as to a member of the staff, or rather a member of the family because this is a restaurant in the South of France of the usual village kind where the employees are all descendant from the chef father and the hostess mother to sons and daughters and even grandchildren who come by on their velos to eat and help clear tables, after school.

The parrot's plumage is green and yellow, with a touch of red somewhere, a grey curved beak that, because the creature's been there as long as the founding habitués at their tables, seems to have aged that way like some old man's nose. English tourists and those retired from their cold shires, by their culture amateur ornithologists, know that the parrot is African, and also know him by name, Auguste. But the most constant clientele, out as well as in season, is local. The older habitués, native and foreign, have seen them, heard them grow up, from the time of baby carriages, the racing past tables chasing balls, to the sexy tattooed biceps, the giggling and flirting over cigarettes, the transformation of bared be-ringed navels to the swelling mounds of pregnancy.

In season the parrot in his domed cage is outdoors under a tree on the territory of the *Place* where the restaurant spreads its tables and umbrellas. Out of season he is thrust away with summer in a corner of the restaurant if the weather is bad; a sort of hibernation imposed on him that is surely contrary to the cycle of his species, wherever its origin. Sometimes there's even his night-time cloth thrown over the roof of his cage. Take a nap. But most of the year, in that mild climate, he is at his post outdoors in the middle of the day, and clients favour eating there. —Auguste! Hullo!— People call out as they stroll to be seated. —Auguste! Bon jour!— As if they must be acknowledged by him, the sign, the character of their choice of where to eat and drink, as some feel prestige in being recognised by a *maître d'hôtel*. And with the assertion of dignity of a *maître d'* sometimes he calls back or murmurs in that mysterious throat of his, Hullo bon jour. Sometimes not. He pretends to be busy attending to some displacement of his plumage or shifting the precise prehensile grip of his claws. They, like his beak, have taken on the human characteristics of the clients beyond his cage but long around him—the skin of the claws of his kind of hands furrowed, hardened, cross-wrinkled by mutual ageing.

Parents send their children from the tables to greet him. Go and see the parrot, say something to it, it can talk, you know. So the adults get rid of infant chatter and whining. Don't put your finger through the bars! This's not a kittycat! Go—see that parrot over there?

The children surround the cage and stare. His half-lidded insignificant eyes—he is all beak, all the attribute of what takes food and utters—look back at them as a public figure endures the sameness of the face of the crowd. He won't speak although mummy and daddy say so and what mummy and daddy say must be true. Right. Auguste is presumed to be a male because of his raucous voice: suddenly he obliges with raging shrieks, the yells of a street fight. Some children run away, others laugh and tease him for more. It's as if inappropriate violence has brought an unsuitable reminder to the pleasant security of choosing from the menu with the member of the chef's family offering advice of the specials of the day. Madame Delancy may even come out, shrugging and smiling, gently to direct the taunting children away. Perhaps she has the segment of a tangerine or an open mussel in her fingers to soothe the bird. (When clients are astonished at the spectacle of a parrot enjoying *moules marinières* she cocks her head and says—iodine—maybe that's why he lives so long.) He will take the titbit and continue to grumble with quiet indignation to himself, while apparently listening acutely to all around him, for as suddenly as he flew into a rage he enters unbidden across all the conversations the clichés of his vocabulary over the clichés of theirs. —Santé cheers wha-tt! really? well-l so! so-oo ça va? come on! tu parles! love . . . ly bye now ça va?— All the nuances of hilarity, derision, irritation, disbelief, boredom are faithfully introduced, reproduced. The inflections of what must be called his voice adapt to whether he's having his say in French or English—it seems the advent of German and Scandinavian clients has not, in this latter part of his thirty years, enabled him to reproduce their locutions.

But now there's change coming to the charming village—of course it has kept its character through many changes, longer than the legendary longevity of a parrot. The revolution that sent the monks fleeing from their monastery whose cloisters are now the garden bar of its avatar as a five-star hotel; the German occupation in the 1940s in which young men of village families still extant (look at those baby carriages) were killed in the Resistance—there's a street where one was born, named after him. There has been the restoration of rotting beams in old houses by Scandinavians, Germans and the English, who in the boom years of Europe discovered a delightful unspoilt place to acquire a historic *maison secondaire*.

This latest change has a finality about it—as no doubt they all have had for whoever lived in or visited the village 'as it used to be'. Before. For each individual another 'before'. But one of the finalities, now, is the announced closing of the restaurant of the parrot. After thirty years! Madame Delancy knows she owes an explanation to the habitués, whether the survivors of the lesbian community from the Twenties, the regular summer visitors, or the youngsters who take their right as a species of collateral grandchildren to sit smoking, jeering and chattering for more than an hour over a single coffee or a shared icecream. The chef, her dear husband who (everyone has heard related many times) learned his skills in the kitchens of Maxim's in Paris, has been cooking for more than forty years. For some while they have had a small apartment with a view of the sea, ready in preparation for this time that has come. So the tables with their white napery and flowers, the chairs on which everyone is at ease, raising glasses, all will be folded away, the ice buckets where bottles of Provençal Rosé are powdered with chill, and the chef's incomparable *Tarte Tatin* that is displayed among desserts—all will disappear. No. No? A German gentleman has bought the restaurant. As if one can 'buy' a restaurant whose character has been formed over thirty years. A German. Sauerkraut and sausages. Or worse, something imagined as international French cuisine by those who are not French.

An imperious scream from under a bower. —Bon jour! Bon soir! Hullo! Ça va?— reminds: and Auguste, what will happen to the parrot? Can he be bought along with the premises?

The parrot will move to the apartment. What a question.

But there is a question: what life will it be for him, alone with an old couple gazing at the sea. Oh the family, the children and grandchildren will visit. Sometimes. Everyone has found other work.

The final week of the restaurant's life it is more fully patronised than ever. One must eat there just one time again, it's going to be the last time. For some people: of many phases, stages, stations of lifetime. The parrot has witnessed these; those that people remember, have forgotten, or want to forget. He is particularly talkative during his last chance of recollection declared, it seems that if the creature is long-lived, it also has a relentless memory. It is all there in whatever strange faculty is hidden in that feathered throat and blunt grey tongue behind the probing beak. He laughs the crescendo laugh of a coquettish woman who may or may not hear herself in it as she comes stooping on an invalid's walker to sit for one last lunch at her usual table. Now he's tittering nonsensically from the adolescence of girls who have disappeared into the cities; the parents, eating their ultimate *Daube Provençale*, haven't had news for months. The tittering sweeps away to a drunken blast (that poor devil, relic of former habitués, begs now outside the market). The murmur of lovers across a table (the hostile couple who don't exchange a word while they eat), the insinuating laugh of gossips whose predictions of mismatch and betrayal have come to pass, there—and someone smiling a farewell, cajoling, Auguste, Auguste, turns away from the cage at lack of response, the creature has gone silent. He fidgets about the cage as if to find a bribe of sugar he has missed. But it's more than that. He yells anguish, PAPA PAPA PA—PAA! Where is that child from whom this cry came, and is stored, maybe for the rest of a hundred years? PA—PAA! Where is the father who was called for in desperate appeal, and did he ever come. HULLO HULLO PA—PAAA PA—PAAA! BON JOUR BON SOIR WHAT? WHAT? ÇA VA? ÇA VA? The parroting that isn't only that of parrots repeats how we hide from one another's hurts. ÇA VA?

How goes it.

And from the depths of whatever he has that mocks vocal chords, low and angry, there is what was overheard, what he shouldn't have overheard. *Ça ne va pas du tout.*

Doesn't go at all.

a beneficiary

CACHES of old papers are graves, you shouldn't open them.

Her mother had been cremated. There is no marble page incised Laila de Morne, born, died, actress.

She always lied about her age; it wasn't her natal name, that was too ethnically limiting, inherited generations back, to suggest her uniqueness in a programme cast list. It wasn't her married name, either. She had baptised herself; professionally. She was long divorced although only in her late fifties when a taxi hit her car and (as she would have delivered her last line) brought down the curtain on her career. Her daughter Charlotte has her father's surname and has been close to him as a child can be subject to an ex-husband's conditions of access while the ex-wife, customarily, has custody. As Charlotte has grown up she's felt more compatible with him than with her, fondly though she feels towards her mother's— somehow—childishness. Perhaps acting is really continuing the make-believe games of childhood—fascinating, in a way.

But. But what? Not a way she had wanted to follow. Although named after the character in which her mother had an early success (Charlotte Corday, Peter Weiss's *Marat/Sade*) and despite the encouragement of drama and dance classes. Not a way she could follow because of lack of talent: her mother's unspoken interpretation of disappointment, if not expressed in reproach. Laila de Morne had not committed herself to any lover so far as marrying again. There was no stepfather to confuse relations, loyalties; Charlie (as he called her) could remark to her father, 'Why should she expect me to take after her?'

Her father was a neurologist. They laughed together; at any predestinatory prerogative of the mother, or the alternative paternal one, to be expected to become a doctor! Poking around in people's brains? They nudged one another with the elbowing of more laughter at the daughter's distaste.

Her father helped to arrange the memorial gathering in place of a funeral service, sensitive as always to any need in her life. She certainly wouldn't have expected or wanted him to come along to an ex-wife's apartment and get down to sorting the clothes, personal possessions to be kept or given away. A friend from the firm where she worked as an actuary agreed to help for a free weekend. Unexpectedly, the young civil rights lawyer with whom there had been a sensed mutual attraction taken no further than dinner and a cinema date, offered himself—perhaps a move towards a love affair, which was coming about anyway. The girls emptied the cupboards of clothes, the friend exclaiming over the elaborate range of different styles women of that generation wore, seems they had many personalities to project—as if you could choose, now you belonged to the outfit of jeans and T-shirt. Oh of course! Charlotte's mother was a famous actress!

Charlotte did not correct this out of respect for the ambitions of her mother. But when she went to the next room, where the lawyer was arranging chronologically, for her, press cuttings and programmes, photographs displaying Laila in the roles for which the wardrobe had provided, she turned a few programmes and remarked to be overheard by him rather than to him, 'Never really had the leads she believed she should have after the glowing notices of her promise, very young. When she murdered Marat. In his bathtub, wasn't it. I've never seen the play.' Confiding the truth of her mother's career, betraying Laila's idea of herself; perhaps also a move towards a love affair.

The three young people broke out of trappings of the past for coffee and their concerns of the present. What sort of court cases does a civil rights lawyer take on? What did he mean by not the usual litigation? No robberies, highjacks? Did the two young women feel they were discriminated against, did the plum jobs go to males? Or was it t'other way about, did bad conscience over gender discrimination mean that women were elevated to positions they weren't really up to? Women of any colour; and black men, same thing? What would have been the sad and strange task alone became a lively evening, animated exchange of opinions and experiences.

Laila surely would not have disapproved; she had stimulated her audience.

There was a Sunday evening at a jazz club, sharing enthusiasm and a boredom with hip-hop, kwaito. After a dinner and dancing together, that first bodily contact to confirm attraction, he offered to help again with her task, and on a weekend afternoon they kissed and touched among the stacks of clothes and boxes of theatre souvenirs, his hand brimming with her breast, but did not proceed as would be natural to the beautiful and inviting bed with its signature of draped shawls and cushions. Some atavistic taboo, notion of respect for the dead, as if her mother still lay there in possession.

The love affair found a bed elsewhere and continued uncertainly, pleasurably enough but without much expectation of commitment. A one-act piece begun among the props of a supporting-part career.

Charlotte brushed aside any offers, also from her office friend, to continue with the sorting of Laila's—what? The clothes were packed up, some seemed wearable only in the context of a theatrical wardrobe and were given to an experimental theatre group, others went to the Salvation Army for distribution to the homeless. Her father arranged with an estate agent to advertise the apartment for sale; unless you want to move in, he suggested. It was too big, his Charlie couldn't afford to, didn't want to live in a style not her own, even rent-free. They laughed again in their understanding, not in criticism of her mother. Laila was Laila. He agreed, but as if in relation to some other aspect. Yes, Laila.

The movers came to take the furniture to be sold. She half-thought of inheriting the bed, it would be luxurious to flop diagonally across its generosity; but you wouldn't be able to get it past the bedroom door, in her small flat. When the men had departed with their loads there were pale shapes on the floors where everything had stood. She opened windows to let out the dust, the special atmosphere of an occupation like the air of a cave, and turning back suddenly saw something had been left behind. A couple of empty boxes, the cardboard ones of supermarket delivery. Irritated, she went to gather them;

one wasn't empty. It seemed to be filled with letters. What makes you keep some letters and crumple others for the bin. In her own comparatively short life she'd thrown away giggly schoolgirl stuff, sexy propositions scribbled on the back of menus, once naïvely found flattering, polite letters of rejection in response to a job beyond her qualifications she had applied for—a salutary lesson on what her set called the Real World. This box apparently contained memorabilia different from the other stuff already dealt with. The envelopes had the look of personal letters. Hand-addressed, without printed logos of business, bank. Did Laila have a personal life at all that wasn't her family-the-theatre? One child, daughter of a divorced marriage, hardly counts as 'family'.

Charlotte—that was the identity she had in any context of her mother—sifted over the envelopes. If her mother did have a personal life it was not a material possession to be disposed of like garments taken on and off; a personal life can't be 'left to' a daughter, a beneficiary in a will. Whatever letters Laila chose to keep were still hers; just quietly burn them, as Laila herself was consumed, to join her. They say (read somewhere) nothing no-one ever disappears, up in the atmosphere, strato- sphere, whatever you call space- atoms infinitely minute be- yond conception of existence are up there forever, from the whole world, from all time. Just as she had noticed this one box that was not empty, as she shook it so that the contents would settle and not spill when lifted, she noticed some loose sheets of writing paper face-down. Not held in the privacy of an envelope. She picked them out face-up. Her father's hand- writing. More deliberately formed than Charlie knew it, what was the date at the top of the page under the address of the house she remembered as home when she was a small girl. A date twenty-four years back—of course his handwriting had changed a bit, it does with different stages in one's life. His Charlie is twenty-eight, so she would have been four years old when he wrote the date, that's about right, must have been just before the divorce and her move to a new home with Laila.

The letter is formally addressed on the upper left-hand side of the paper to a firm of lawyers, Kaplan McLeod & Partners, and directed to one of them *Dear Hamish*. Why on earth would Laila want to keep from a dead marriage the sort of business letter a neurologist might have to write on some question of a car accident maybe or non-payment of some patient's consultation fee or surgery charges. (As if her father's medical and human ethics would ever lead him to this last . . .) The pages must have got mixed up with the other, personal material at some time. Laila and Charlotte changed apartments frequently during Charlotte's childhood and adolescence.

The letter is marked 'Copy'.

'My wife Laila de Morne is an actress and in the course of pursuing her career has moved in a circle independent of one shared by a couple in marriage. I have always encouraged her to take the opportunities, through contacts she might make, to further her talent. She is a very attractive woman and it was obvious to me that I should have to accept there would be men, certainly among her fellow actors, who would want to be more than admirers. But while she enjoyed the attention, sometimes responded with the general kind of social flirtation, I had no reason to see this as more than natural pleasure in her own looks and talents. She would make fun of these admirers, privately, to me, sharp remarks on their appearance, their pretentions and if they were actors, directors or playwrights, the quality of their work. I knew I had not married a woman who would want to stay home and nurse babies, but from time to time she would bring up the subject, we ought to have a son, she said, for me. Then she would get a new part in a play and this was understandably postponed. After a successful start her career was however not advancing to her expectations, she had not succeeded in getting several roles she had confidently anticipated. She came home elated one night and told me she had a small part in a play accepted for performance overseas in the Edinburgh Fringe Festival. She had been selected because the leading actor himself, Rendall Harris, had told the casting director she was the most talented of young women in the theatre group. I was happy for her and we gave a farewell party in our house the night before the cast left for the United Kingdom. After Edinburgh she spent some time in London, calling to say how wonderful and necessary it was for her to experience what was happening in theatre there and, I gathered, trying her luck in auditions. Apparently unsuccessfully.

Perhaps she intended not to come back. She did. A few weeks later she told me she had just been to a gynaecologist and confirmed that she was pregnant. I was moved. I took the unlikely luck of conception—I'd assumed when we made love the night of the party she'd taken the usual precautions, we weren't drunk even if she was triumphant—as a symbol of what would be a change in our perhaps unsuitable marriage. I am a medical specialist, neurological surgeon.

When the child was born it looked like any other red-faced infant but after several months everyone was remarking how the little girl was the image of Laila, the mother. It was one day, a Saturday afternoon when she was kicking and flinging her arms athletically, we were admiring our baby's progress, her beauty, and I joked "Lucky she doesn't look like me" that my wife picked her up, away, and told me "She's not your child." She'd met someone in Edinburgh. I interrupted with angry questions. No, she prevaricated, all right, London, the affair began in London. The leading actor who had insisted on her playing the small part introduced her to someone there. A few days later she told: it was not "someone" it was the leading actor. He was the father of our girl child. She told this to other people, our friends, as through the press it became news that the actor Rendall Harris was making a big name for himself in plays by Tom Stoppard and Tennessee Williams.

I couldn't decide what to believe. I even consulted a colleague in the medical profession about the precise variations in the period of gestation in relation to birth. Apparently it was possible that the conception could have taken place with me, or with the other man a few days before, or after, intercourse with me. There never was any intention expressed by Laila that she would take the child and make her life with the man. She was too proud to let anyone know that the fact probably was that he didn't want her or the supposed progeny of one of his affairs.

Laila has devoted herself to her acting career and as a result the role of a father has of necessity led to a closer relation than customary with the care of the small girl, now four years old. I am devoted to her and can produce witnesses to the conviction that she would be happiest in my custody.

I hope this is adequate. Let me know if anything more is needed, or if there is too much detail. I'm accustomed to writing reports in medical jargon and thought this should be very different. I don't suppose I've a hope in hell of getting Charlie, Laila will put all her dramatic skills into swearing isn't mine.'

THAT Saturday. It landed in the apartment looted by the present filled it with blasting amazement, the presence of the past. That Saturday just as it had come to him. Charlotte/Charlie (what was she) received exactly as he had, what Laila (yes, her mother, giving birth is proof) had told.

How to recognise something not in the vocabulary of your known emotions. Shock is like a ringing in the ears, to stop it you snatch back to the first page, read the letter again. It said what is said. This sinking collapse from within, from flared breathless nostrils down under breasts, stomach, legs and hands, hands that not only feel passively but go out to grasp what can't be. Dismay that feeble-sounding word has this ghastly meaning. What do you do with something you've been Told? Something that now is there in the gut of your existence. Run to him. Thrust his letter at him, at her—but she's out of it, she's escaped in smoke from the crematorium. And she's the one who really knows—knew.

Of course he didn't get custody. He was awarded the divorce decree but the mother was given the four-year-old child. It is natural, particularly in the case of a small girl, for a child to live with the mother. In spite of this 'deposition' of his in which he is denied paternity he paid maintenance for the child. The expensive boarding school, the drama and dance classes, even those holidays in the Seychelles, three times in Spain, once in France, once in Greece, with the mother. Must have paid generously. He was a neurologist more successful in his profession than the child's mother was on the stage. But this couldn't be the reason for the generosity.

Charlotte/Charlie couldn't think about that either. She folded the two sheets, fumbled absently for an envelope they should have been in, weren't, and with them in her hand left the boxes, the letters, Laila's apartment, locked, behind the door.

HE can only be asked: why he's been a father, loving.

The return of his Saturday, it woke her at three, four in the morning when she had kept it at bay through the activities of the day, work, navigating alone in her car the city's crush, mustn't be distracted, leisure occupied in the company of friends who haven't been Told. She and her father had one of their regular early dinners at his favourite restaurant, went on to a foreign movie by a director whose work she admired and the Saturday couldn't be spoken: was unreal.

In the dark when the late-night traffic was over and the dawn traffic hadn't begun: silence.

The reason.

He believed in the one chance of conception that single night of the party. Laila's farewell. Even though his friend expert in biological medicine said, implying if one didn't know the stage of the woman's fertility cycle you couldn't be sure, the conception might have achieved itself in other intercourse a few days before or even after that unique night. I am Charlie, his.

The reason.

Another night-thought; angry mood—who do they think

they are deciding who I am to suit themselves, her vanity, she at least can bear *the child* of an actor with a career ahead in the theatre she isn't attaining for herself, he in wounded macho pride refusing to accept another male's potency. His seed *has* to have been the winner.

And in the morning, before the distractions of the day take over, shame on herself, Charlie, for thinking so spitefully, cheaply about him.

The next reason that offers itself is hardly less unjust, offensive—confusedly hurtful to her, as whatever it is that comes, called up by her. He paid one kind of maintenance, he paid another kind of maintenance, loving her, to keep up the conventions before what he sees as the world. The respectable doctors in their white coats who have wives to accompany them to medical council dinners. If he had married again it would have been a woman like these. Laila was Laila. Never risk another.

The letter that didn't belong to anyone's daughter was moved from place to place, in a drawer under sweaters, an Indian box where she kept earrings and bracelets, behind books of plays, Euripides and Racine, Shaw to Brecht, Dario Fo, Miller, Artaud, Beckett, and of course Weiss's annotated *Marat/Sade*; Charlotte's inheritance, never read.

When you are in many minds, the contention makes someone who has been not quite what one wanted, who doesn't count, the only person to be Told. In bed, yet another night, after love-making when the guards go down with the relaxed physical tensions. Dale, the civil rights lawyer who didn't act in the mess of divorce litigation unless this infringed Constitutional Rights, told in turn of the letter: 'Tear it up.' When she appealed, it was not just a piece of paper—'Have a DNA test.' How to do that without taking the whole cache that was the past to the father. 'Get a snip of his hair.' All that's needed to go along with a sample of her blood. Like who was it in the bible cutting off Samson's beard. How was she supposed to do that, stealing upon the father in his sleep somewhere?

Tear it up. Easy advice from someone who had understood nothing. She did not.

But a circumstance came about as if somehow summoned . . . Of course, it was fortuitous . . . A distinguished actor-director had been invited by a local theatre to direct a season of classical and avant-garde plays, taking several lead roles himself. It was his first return to the country, the city where he was born and had left to pursue his career, he said in newspaper interviews and on radio, television—how long?—oh twenty-five years ago. Rendall Harris. Newspaper photographs: an actor's assumed face for many cameras, handsomely enough late-middle-aged, defiant slight twist to the mouth to emphasise character, eyebrows heightened together amusedly just above nose, touch of white in short sideburns. Eyes are not clearly to be made out on newsprint. On television, alive; something of the upper body, gestures coming into view, the close-up of changing expressions in the face, the actual meeting with deep-set long eyes, grey darkening by some deliberate intensity almost flashing-black, to yours, the viewer's. What did she expect, a recognition. Hers of him. His, out of the lit-up box, of her. An actor's performance face.

She can't ignore the stir at the idea that the man named by her mother is about in the city. Laila was Laila. Yes. If she had not gone up in smoke would he have met her, remembered her. Did he ever see the baby, the child was two before he went off for twenty-five years. What does a two-year-old remember.

Has she ever seen this man in a younger self, been taken in by these strikingly interrogative eyes; received.

She was accustomed to go to the theatre with friends of the lawyer-lover although he preferred films, one of his limited tastes she could at least share. Every day—every night—she thought about the theatre. Not with Dale. Not to sit beside any of her friends. No. For a wild recurrent impulse there was the temptation to be there with her father, who did not know she knew, had been Told as he was that Saturday, passed on to her in the letter under volumes of plays. Laila was Laila. For him and for her.

She went alone when Rendall Harris was to play one of the lead roles. There had been ecstatic notices. He was Laurence Olivier reincarnated for a new, the twenty-first, century, a deconstructed style of performance. She was far back in the box office queue when a board went up, House Full. She booked for another night, online, an aisle seat three rows from the proscenium. She found herself at the theatre, for some reason hostile. Ridiculous. She wanted to disagree with the critics. That's what it was about.

Rendall Harris—how do you describe a performance that manages to create for his audience the wholeness, the life of a man, not just in 'character' for the duration of the play, but what he might have been before those events chosen by the playwright and how he'll be, alive, continuing after. Rendall Harris is an extraordinary actor: man. Her palms were up in the hands applauding like a flight of birds rising. When he came out to take the calls summoning the rest of the cast round him she wasn't in his direct eye-line as she would have been if she'd asked for a middle of the row seat.

She went to every performance in which he was billed in the cast. A seat in the middle of the second row, the first would be too obvious.

If she was something other than a groupie, she was among the knot of autograph seekers, one night, who hung about the foyer hoping he might leave the theatre that way. He did appear making for the bar with the theatre director and for a moment under the arrest of programmes thrust at him happened to encounter her eyes as she stood back from his fans—a smile of self-deprecating amusement meant for anybody in the line of vision, but that one was she.

The lift of his face, his walk, his repertoire of gestures, the oddities of lapses in character-cast expression on stage that she secretly recognised as himself appearing, became almost familiar to her. As if she somehow knew him and these intimacies knew her. Signals. If invented, they were very like conviction. The more she ignored it: kept on going to take her place in the second row. At the box office there was the routine question, D'you have a season ticket? Suppose that was to have been bought when the Rendall Harris engagement was announced.

She thought to herself, a letter. Owed it to him for the impression his roles made upon her. His command of the drama of *living*, the excitement of being there with him. With the fourth or fifth version up in her mind, the next was written. Mailed to the theatre it most likely was glanced through in his dressing room or back at his hotel among other 'tributes' and either would be forgotten or might be taken back to London for his collection of the memorabilia boxes it seems actors needed. But with him, there was that wry sideways tilt to the photographed mouth.

Of course she neither expected nor had any acknowledgement.

After a performance one night she bumped into some old friends of Laila, actors who had come to the memorial gathering, and they insisted on her joining them in the bar. When Rendall Harris's unmistakable head appeared through the late crowd, they created a swift current past backs to embrace him, draw him with their buddie the theatre director to room made at the table where she had been left among the bottles and glasses. For her this was—he had to be taken as an exchange of bar-table greetings; the friends, in the excitement of having Rendall Harris among themselves forgot to introduce her as Laila's daughter, Laila who'd played Corday in that early production where'd he'd been Marat; perhaps they have forgotten Laila, best thing with the dead if you want to get on with your life and ignore the hazards, like that killer taxi, around you. Her letter was no more present than the other one under the volumes of plays. A fresh acquaintance, just the meeting of a nobody with the famous. Not entirely, even from the famous actor's side. As the talk lobbed back and forth, sitting almost opposite her the man thought it friendly, from his special level of presence, to toss something to a young woman no-one was including, and easily found what came to mind: 'Aren't you the one who's been sitting bang in the middle of the second row, several times lately?' And then they joined in laughter, a double confession, hers of absorbed concentration on him, his of being aware of it or at least becoming so at the sight, here, of someone out there whose attention had caught him. He asked across the voices of others which plays in the repertoire she's enjoyed best, what criticisms she had of those she didn't think much of. He named a number she hadn't seen; her response made clear another confession—she'd seen only those in which he played a part. When the party broke up and all were meandering their way, with stops and starts in back-chat and laughter, to the foyer, a shift in progress brought gesturing Rendall Harris's back right in front of her—he turned swiftly, lithely as a young man and, must have been impulse in one accustomed to be natural, charming in spite of professional guard, spoke as if he had been thinking of it: 'You've missed a lot, you know, so flattering for me, avoiding the other plays. Come some night, or there's a Sunday afternoon performance of a Wole Soyinka you ought to see. We'll have a bite in the restaurant before I take you to your favourite seat. I'm particularly interested in audience reaction to the big chances I've taken directing this play.'

Rendall Harris sits beside her through the performance, now and then with the authority to whisper some comment, drawing her attention to this and that. She's told him, over lasagne at lunch, that she's an actuary, that creature of calculation, couldn't be further from qualification to judge the art of actors' interpretation or that of a director. 'You know that's not true.' Said with serious inattention. Tempting to accept that he senses something in her blood, sensibility. From her mother. It is or is not the moment to tell him she is Laila's daughter, although she carries Laila's husband's name, Laila was not known by.

Now what sort of a conundrum is that supposed to be? She was produced by what was that long term, parthenogenesis, she just growed, like Topsy? You know that's not true.

He arranged for her seat as his guest for the rest of the repertoire in which he was playing the lead. It was taken for granted she'd come backstage afterwards. Sometimes he included her in other cast gatherings 'among people your own age' obliquely acknowledging his own, old enough to be her father. Cool. He apparently had no children, adult or otherwise, didn't mention any. Was he gay? Now? Does a man change sexual preference, or literally embrace both. As he played so startlingly, electric with the voltage of life the beings created only in words by Shakespeare, Strindberg, Brecht, Beckett—oh you name them from the volumes holding down the letter telling of that Saturday. 'You seem to understand what I—we—actors absolutely risk, kill themselves, trying to reach the ultimate identity in what's known as a character, beating ourselves down to let the creation take over. Haven't you ever wanted to have a go, yourself? Thought about acting?' She told: 'I know an actuary is the absolute antithesis of all that. I don't have the talent.' He didn't make some comforting effort. Didn't encourage magnanimously, why not have a go. 'Maybe you're right. Nothing like the failure of an actor. It isn't like many other kinds of failure, it doesn't just happen inside you, it happens before an audience. Better be yourself. You're a very interesting young woman, depths there, I don't know if you know it—but I think you do.'

Like every sexually attractive young woman she was experienced in the mostly pathetic drive ageing men have towards them. Some of the men are themselves attractive either because they have somehow kept the promise of vigour, mouths with their own teeth, tight muscular buttocks in their jeans, no jowls, fine eyes that have seen much to impart, or because they're well-known, distinguished, well yes, even rich. This actor whose enduring male beauty is an attribute of his talent, he is probably more desirable than when he was a novice Marat in Peter Weiss's play; all the roles he has taken, he's emerged from the risk with a strongly endowed identity. Although there is no apparent reason why he should not be making the usual play towards this young woman, there's no sign that he is doing so. She knows the moves; they are not being made.

The attention is something else. Between them. Is this a question or a fact? They wouldn't know, would they. The other, simple thing is he welcomes her like a breeze come in with this season abroad, in his old home town; seems to refresh him. Famous people have protégés; even if it's that he takes, as the customary part of his multiply responsive public reception. He's remarked, sure to be indulged, he wants to go back to an adventure, a part of the country he'd been thrilled by as a child, wants to climb there where there were great spiky plants with red candelabras—it was the wrong season, these wouldn't be in bloom in this, his kind of season, but she'd drive him there; he took up the shy offer at once and left the cast without him for two days when the plays were not those in which he had his lead. They slipped and scrambled up the peaks he remembered and at the lodge in the evening he was recognised, took this inevitably, autographed bits of paper and quipped privately with her that he was mistaken by some for a pop star he hadn't heard of but ought to have. His unconscious vitality invigorated people around him wherever he was. No wonder he was such an innovative director; the critics wrote that classic plays, even the standbys of Greek drama, were re-imagined as if this was the way they were meant to be and never had been before. It wasn't in his shadow, she was: in his light. As if she were re-imagined by herself. He was wittily critical at other people's expense and so with him she was freed to think—say—what she realised she found ponderous in those she worked with, the predictability among her set of friends she usually tolerated without stirring them up. Not that she saw much of friends at present. She was part of the cast of the backstage scene. A recruit to the family of actors in the coffee shop at lunch, privy to their gossip, their bantering with the actor-director who drew so much from them, roused their eager talent. The regular Charlie dinners with her father, often postponed, were subdued, he caught this from her; there wasn't much for them to talk about. Unless she were to want to show off her new associations.

The old impulse came, unwelcome, to go with him to the theatre. Suppressed. But returned. Sit with him and see the one commanding on the stage. What for? Would this resolve, she is Charlotte not Charlie.

Buried under the weight of books, there came out—Charlie said, 'Let's see the play that's had such rave reviews, I'll get tickets.' He didn't demur, forgotten who Randell Harris was; might be.

He led to the bar afterwards talking of the play with considering interest—he'd not seen Beckett for ages, it wore well, not outdated. She didn't want to be there, she urged it was late, no, no, she didn't want a drink, the bar was too crowded, but he persuaded gently, we won't stay, I'm thirsty, need a beer. The leading actor was in a spatter of applause over the drinks as he moved about the salute of admiration. He talked through clusters of others and arrived.

'Rendall, my father.'

'Congratulations. Wonderful performance, the critics don't exaggerate.'

The actor—he dismissed the laudation as if he had enough of that from people who don't understand what such an interpretation of Vladimir or Estragon involves, the (what was that word he always used) risk. 'I didn't feel right tonight. I was missing a beat. Charlotte, you've seen me do better, hey, m'darling.' Her father picked up his glass but didn't drink. 'Last time I saw you was in the play set in an asylum, Laila de Morne was Charlotte Corday.'

Her father Told.

'Of course you always get chalked up in the critics' hierarchy by how you play the classics, but I'm more fascinated by the new stuff, movement-theatre, parts I can take from zero. I've sat in that bathtub too many times, knifed by Charlotte Cordays . . .'. The projection of the disarmingly self-deprecating laugh.

She spoke what she had not Told, not yet found the right time and situation to say to him. 'Laila de Morne is my mother.' No more to be discarded in the past tense than the performance of the de Sade asylum where she was Charlotte Corday to his Marat. 'That's how I was named.' 'Well, you're sure not a Charlotte to carry a knife, spoil your beautiful aura with that, frighten off the men around you.' Peaked eyebrows as if, ruefully, one of them, a trick from the actors' repertoire contradicted by a momentary—hardly to be received— entrance of those eyes to her own, diamonds black with the intensity it was his talent to summon, a stage-prop claim made, to be at once released, at will.

Laila was Laila.

WHEN they were silent in the pause at a traffic light he touched the open shield of his palm to the back of her head, the unobtrusive caress used the times he was driving her to boarding school. If she was for her own reasons now differently disturbed that was not to be pried at. She was to drop him at his apartment, but when she drew up at the entrance she opened the car door at her side as he did his, and came to him in the street. He turned—what's the matter. She moved her head: nothing. She went to him and he saw without understanding he must take her in his arms. She held him, he kissed her cheek and she pressed it against his. Nothing to do with DNA.

alternative endings

ASKED about how fiction writers bring their imagined characters to life, Graham Greene said writers create alternative lives for people they might have encountered, sat beside on a bus, overheard in loving or quarrelsome exchange on a beach, in a bar, grinning instead of weeping at a funeral, shouting at a political meeting (my examples).

A writer also picks up an imagined life at some stage in the human cycle and leaves it at another. Not even a story from birth to death is decisive; what mating, by whom, brought about the entry, what consequences follow the exit—these are part of the story that hasn't been chosen to be told. The continuity of existence has to be selectively interrupted by the sense of form which is art. In particular, when we come to close a story, it ends This Way, that's the writer's choice according to what's been revealed to the writer of the personality, the known reactions, emotions, sense of self in the individuals created. But couldn't it have ended That Way? Might not the moment, the event, the realisation have been received differently, meant something other to the individual, that the writer didn't think, receive intuition of. No matter how cumulative, determinative, obvious even, the situation could be, might it not find its resolution differently? This way, not that. There is choice in the unpredictability of humans; the forms of story-telling are arbitrary. There are alternative endings. I've tried them out, here, for myself.

the first sense

The senses 'usually reckoned as five—sight, hearing, smell, taste, touch.'

—*Oxford English Dictionary*

H E has to make a living any way he can.

He was a young D.Phil from Budapest—then, when they emigrated for reasons nobody here is interested in; there have been so many waves of Europeans, whites moving in on the blacks' country. Whether this time the instance was escape from communist rule or the one that succeeded it, in Hungary, is too remote. Soon the country of adoption went through an overturn of regime of its own; victory and the different problems unvisioned that presents, preoccupied the population long programmed to see themselves only as black and white. As for professional opportunities an immigrant hopes for in a new land—what university could have been expected to appoint a professor who was fluent at academic level only in a remote language, with the ability to speak one other— German—well enough maybe to lecture where this was on the curricula of European tongues in a country that itself had a Tower of Babel: eleven official languages, after the change of regime.

In the obligation of natal solidarity, someone of an older generation of immigrants, whose children were conceived and born in South Africa, arranged for the member of new immigration to be employed in the prosperous sons' supermarket. Stores Department. Ferenc became Fred.

It's not a bad living. The pay modest; what one would expect for the working-class. He was a storeman; Stores Manager now, with a team of young black assistants careening hugely loaded trolleys about with the power of splendid muscles raised on the soccer fields. Strangely—a well-educated man would be expected to have the advantage of facility in learning a new language he hears spoken about him every day—his English has never advanced beyond the simple colloquial vocabulary of supermarket exchanges. So moving up to some level of activity, even commercial if not intellectual, commensurate with any career he would have had back where he came from, faded as a promise, a possibility. She—Zsuzsana—who had no more than schooling in a small Hungarian town, picked up the language easily; perhaps perforce, because having been taught how to sew in accordance with the strict requirements of a female role imposed by her grandmother, had turned resourcefully to dressmaking as the way to contribute to getting ends meet. She had become fluent in order to speak her clients' language in flattery of their appearance. The child born to the couple in immigration (both felt, what better way to make claim to a new country) went to school where the language of instruction and of his playmates was English. *Peter.* A name chosen common to many countries, distinguishable only by differing pronunciation. The boy and his mother chattered away in English together, at home. Magyar, like Latin in churches, belonged in a special context, undertones spoken on the occasions of love-making.

For the first years Ferenc had friends, still back there, send him newspapers. But reading, here, what was happening in Hungary, what crowds were demanding of whatever new government, what was being discussed in the endless forum of Budapest cafés became detached from the venue, abstract, without accompanying vision, awareness of familiar place. This was the reverse of looking at old photographs, recognising the place in which they were taken and having no memory of who the people were. It was Fred, driving in his Korean car across the vast suspension bridge—named for this country's great hero, Mandela—who was suddenly crossing from Buda to Pest over the gleaming breast of the Danube, and not over the confusion of railroad tracks the hero's bridge actually spans. Budapest. The light of the water was in his eyes, the features of faces met him. He was there for the moments of the traverse, being recognised, claimed by the façades, the detailed prospects of streets rising from the river-of-rivers. He *saw*. As he did not see any other place.

His enterprising, hard-working wife had more women coming to be clothed by her than she could 'take on' as she said in quick-witted acquisition of their turns of phrase, their vision of themselves, their scattering of the word 'darling' as punctuation of what neckline, what brief scrap of skirt, there in the mirror, would 'make the best of what I've got to show, darling'. They stayed for her coffee after a fitting. Unlike a man, a woman in her difference, her foreign image, is attractive to locals, doesn't have to conform to some other norm. Her name was not translated into something less exotic. The abbreviation of Zsuzsana, 'Zsuzsi', by which she'd been known since childhood, sounded like the familiar 'Susie', common in English. An evening dress, a pants suit made by Zsuzsi caught a certain touch of European fashion flair that couldn't be bought off the peg. She had a little assistant to iron the seams and tack the hems, a young black girl, as he had his black team of muscle to man the trolleys.

IT was through her friendly relations with her clients that it came about.

AS the women for whose image she sewed were inclined to take someone outside their social circle into confidences over their lives she was herself beguiled in turn to confess, with alert precaution of assuring she enjoyed the privilege of making beautiful clothes for the confidante present, that she was tired of working at home. It wasn't what she was made for; she let it be imagined what that might be. Circumstances kept her shut away from the world. She had 'had enough'—just as the women phrased it, for her unlikely ear alone, of their drug-addict daughter or the second husband who was more difficult than the first. The mother of that daughter was one who had no complaints about a husband, indeed proud of getting a man she believed her own qualities deserved. One of these was her willingness to help others, which her capable husband in the building industry indulged. Perhaps they were good Christians, or good Jews. His firm specialised in restoring grand neglected houses for new-rich people who aspired to the power and prestige of Old Money the image of such mansions recalled. It was easy enough for her; she had the kind idea that the personality, the appearance of Zsuzsi could go into the business of selling such houses—there was the obvious cachet of a European background, the palimpsest images of familiarity with cultured settings far above local standards. The husband introduced the charming Zsuzsi to an estate-agent friend who agreed to give her a trial once reassured that her English was fluent, even advantageously distinguished from the usual *spiel* of estate agents by the occasional Continental flourish—as the accent wasn't German perhaps it was French. She looked good. Well, keep your hands to yourself. She was assigned to a section of the Agency's upmarket territory, those old suburbs from the days of early gold-mining magnates the latest generation of wealthy whites hunted for tradition that wasn't political, just aesthetic, not to be misinterpreted, in assertive frontage and form, as nostalgia for lost white racist supremacy. The Agency's other upmarket activity was where the emergent black jet-set looked to take possession of fake Bauhaus and California haciendas that had been the taste of the final generation of whites in power, the deposed, many of whom had taken their money and gone to Australia or Canada where the Aborigines and the Red Indians had been effectively dealt with.

She worked hard indeed, it seemed to him, who left the Stores warehouse at the same time every weekday morning and returned at the same time every evening. Even longer hours than she had sat at the sewing machine, its whirrs, snipped-off stops and starts that had accompanied Sundays while he sat reading this country's newspapers with its particular political obsessions resultant from its history he didn't share, scenes he couldn't visualise, and the boy entrancedly mimed American shrieks and howls of heroes and villains he was watching on TV. There are no regular hours in the business of selling houses. Prospective buyers and sellers expect the agent to be at their disposal in the evenings and over weekends, whenever it suits the one who is in the market, so to speak. She could hardly oppose with personal inconvenience: 'My husband is waiting for me to cook dinner' he proposed, laughing at presumption of an agent's life being measured against the client's. You don't have to be a philosopher to know immigration means accepting the conditions declared if you want to survive. He and Peter, helpful little lad, put together the meal, frying eggs or heating up the goulash she'd frozen after preparing early some morning—not often the chance for such tasks, some clients want to view houses before going to their offices, legal chambers or doctors' consulting rooms. And it's true that it's a good time to take them viewing, have them come upon a fine house in the fresh light, as a face that may be destined to become familiar, owned. Late-afternoon client viewing appointments would extend into evening, particularly, she learnt and related to him, if things were going well, she could sense that the client's interest in a particular property was rising; advantage must be taken of this by continuing discussion relaxed over a drink in some elegant hotel bar. If she arrived back from these other houses only when the meal father and son had concocted was greasy-cold, it didn't matter: she felt the deal was done. He heated up food for her. She would smile to him, almost nervously, for acknowledgement: commission on the sale of such a prime property was going to be higher than she, without qualifications for any profession, could ever have expected to gain, any way, any place.

The money she was bringing in eased some of the stringencies in their life. Peter had fine sports equipment he had yearned for, the old car was traded in for a later second-hand model and now was Fred's exclusively—the Agency provided Zsuzsi with a car that would give clients confidence in her income status as high enough to be informed of the expectations of their own. But funds didn't extend to provide for major changes in their life—she had to spend considerably on being well-dressed (no time for homemade outfits), groomed, visits to an expensive hairdressing *salon*, including manicure, people notice proletarian hands as a sign of limitations. Of course she had the luck to be good-looking, right basis for being produced by these methods as exceptionally so.

They made a handsome couple when it was assumed, on occasion, husbands, wives, or gay partners of the Agency personnel would get together for the obligatory Christmas party, or some cocktail hour to mark particular progress in the business. He did not know the personal incumbents of Zsuzsi's colleagues, beyond these encounters, well enough to discover what range of topics they might have in common to talk about; except sports events. In this country even women shared this *lingua franca*. Spectator passion for team sports is the only universal religion. Its faithful adherents are everywhere; he was a football centre-forward as a student somewhere else but the litany held good; he followed the matches on fields locally and internationally and could give all the responses. There were the lunches among the agents only, with professional concerns to be discussed 'in house'; anyway lunch break at the supermarket didn't allow time for such leisurely customs. Fred ate in the canteen, or picked up something more to his taste in the deli section where there were hams and spiced sausage imported from Italy and other European countries. Zsuzsi said, yes, good idea, when he once suggested, after mother and son had spent a happily riotous half-hour teasing each other in South African English slang, that they should speak to the boy a short time every day, even round a meal, in Magyar. So that he would have it. It turned out meals were not a suitable choice, the boy was tired after a day at school, play, homework. She didn't have other spare time.

He began to speak their language to the boy without explanation while they were absorbed together in the things fathers are drawn into by young sons—construction with plastic building kits, articulating bodies of battery-operated outerspace monsters. The child spoke unawaringly the Magyar word for 'leg', 'face', used the verbs for 'fly', 'shoot'. But he resented that the creativity he wanted to share with his father was turning into another kind of homework when his father tried to get him to put the words into a sentence, repeating this as it came from his father's voice. He'd suddenly kick over the half-finished creation, scatter the weapons and cloak of the monster, laughing angrily.

Photographs that had been brought in the baggage of emigration and had sifted away somewhere in immigration: when they were shown to the boy so that he might make the words material, come to life in images—'That's our house'—he was only half-attentive. 'Our house isn't like that.' 'It's my house, where I lived when I was like you. A little boy.' Of course, the turret and balustrade would seem to him a picture in a book of fairy tales—but this generation of kids don't have Grimm read to them . . . he wouldn't even have that vision, to match.

Murmured to in the real intimacy of a mother tongue in bed, Zsuzsi wasn't aware she was responding softly in English. Well. She had been speaking in that essential other tongue all

day, showing prospective clients the features of living-places
that if grander, were like those in the familiar images the boy
had; been born among.

Zsuzsi was more more and more successful. Perhaps this
was 'what she was made for' that she couldn't define when she
knew she had enough of being the ladies' little dressmaker.
This was the proof that if there is something in you which
wasn't recognised, the political situation and economic order
had no place for, where you came from, it's true that there are
opportunities to realise your potential, build yourself a life
with the kit of values of another society. She invested some of
her high commissions in the stock market, on the expert advice of stockbrokers who felt they owed to her sensitivity and
native shrewdness (these Eastern Europeans), her reading of
their ambitions, calculated status, the finding of the material
image, the statement of a home that would announce this, unmistakable as a fox has its lair to distinguish it, an ordinary
rich pig its sty. Fred could not take leave from the supermarket at Christmas, when Peter was on holiday from school and
the estate agency more or less idle in the absence of clients—
gone sailing or abroad to snow countries, skiing. So she took
Ferenc and Peter to a Club Méditerranée on an Indian Ocean
island at another time of year, when the availability of all three
made this possible—one of the many treats she provided.

The Agency had become alert to the development opportunity of a change in currency-law restrictions that now allowed
nationals of the country to own property abroad, which had
been illegal for decades. Zsuzsi went back; not to the countries
the Danube flowed through but to France, Spain, England, on
a visit apparently with several colleagues from the Agency to
make contact with famous ones like Christie's and Sotheby's

for co-operation in finding properties for clients interested in a *pied-à-terre* if not a castle in Spain. She came back with T-shirts for the son, picturing famous sights, Gaudí in Barcelona, Houses of Parliament in London, and CDs made by the latest rave bands. The boy didn't ask about the identity of what he saw was going to be displayed across his chest. The CDs overjoyed him. He was older now and did his homework clamped between headphones accompanying him with the sounds of the different kinds of pop music—how could the child concentrate? But his mother said, amused, we can't live in the past, they say even cows give more milk when music's played to them.

But that's Mozart. Ferenc coming up from incarceration in Fred, correcting an incomplete quotation.

HIS Zsuzsi had—what?—some kind of conscience over the unfairness though it was no fault of hers—the traditional social distortion of emigration had thrust a Doctor of Philosophy into a supermarket storeroom—that he had not got out of there, as when they moved to something better she found for them, she had left behind in the little house that was their first shelter in Africa, the sewing machine. Again through resource of client contacts, this time the Agency, at some stage in her success she broached to him that maybe there was some position—well, with his education—in what her clients called the advisory echelons of big business. Such firms were wanting to move into world enterprise. He could do some kind of the research they required?

He wasn't an economist.

Somewhere in her was buried the small-town girl who saw

the distinction attained by the Budapest graduate in philosophy as a Tree of Knowledge fruitful along any branch. He was touched by this returned glimpse of her; vivid vision of how she looked, which was how *she was*, essential self getting up to dance, belonging in the images of the musicians' wild tossing hair, the twisting bodies, limbs rearticulated like Picasso's arrangement of body parts, by a ceiling wheel of turning lights in a student night haunt he'd taken her to.

She did try a few other possibilities for him; nothing had come of them so far. It seemed the initiative for one was from a client not for whom Zsuzsi had found an ideal home but who was a seller of one, his with sauna as well as swimming pool, guest apartment and secure parking for three cars, for which she had found a buyer at top asking price while what other agencies had told the seller was impossibly high. On triumphant first-name terms with his agent, he extended the assumption to the husband, inviting Zsuzsi and Fred to dinner in this successfully overvalued home before he vacated it. For what reason and for where next, if Zsuzsi knew, it was not Fred's business to ask, and did not interest Ferenc. Zsuzsi showed him round. What he saw was that the house was, in fact, beautiful, an interior expressing what must have been someone's sense of what his or hers—their?—containment was meant to be: the eyes met with well-made objects of use, and of visual pleasure—the vista opening from doors as well as the drawings by European artists—Dufy and Braque, lithographs probably—confidently along with the three-dimensional assertion of African wooden sculptures. But the vision might have been the wife's, Zsuzsi had sometime remarked that the man was divorced, or perhaps she said was in the process of divorce.

So this was the kind of scene, background to her life that she—his Zsuzsi—moved through every day. Property to property, kitchen gleamingly equipped as, maybe, a surgeon's operating theatre, deep rooms interleading, wide staircase, bar, patio. He's never seen it before, but it was hers. Connection to the supermarket. The asparagus and scampi to follow, served at dinner by a black man in white jacket, probably came from the cooling chamber for delicate vegetables and the freeze room, where other black men steered loads in wild trajectories and the storeman manager in his open booth surveyed the scene.

The man had room for a boat as well as three cars in his garage. He also had a young son, Zsuzsi said, and he thought it would be nice for Peter to go sailing, on a Sunday, with him and his boy. Peter was half-excited, half-dubious: I don't know them. His mother went along to see him enjoying himself in a new activity. The boat was small, his father didn't come, that time or other Sundays when the same party sailed a stretch of dam water, not a river, during the season. When Zsuzsi went, was obliged to go overseas several times—on one trip the largest German tourist company appointed her their representative in Southern Africa—Peter and he did things together; he thought up outings like a visit to the museum of the origin of mankind but the only success, in really diverting the boy, was the live spectacle of a football game. He couldn't picture his father there, in one of the players, as he had pointed out to him on the field the very position his father had had, look, that player out there. The boy saw *himself* grown, in the bright shorts, the boots, the intense flushed face of that man, there.

A sculptured figure stood on a small table near the chair where he sat reading when he came from the supermarket

evenings while she was away. It was a dignitary whose decorated carved belly rested on crossed legs seated on a low altar
of some sort, its protruding oval ledge empty of the offering it
was meant for. Picked up, there was on the underside an inscription inked into the wood. King Lukengu Tribe Bakuba
Province Kasai. If he glanced up from his book, he saw it; or
it saw him. It was a gift from the client of the farewell dinner
invitation. Its lidded gaze.

She must have sold many more houses before the result of
that one came about. One night on her return from a trip or
was it what she had announced as a weekend conference in
some out-of-town centre, she said, Ferenc, we must talk. She
had picked up the colloquial jargon of the sales-world as she
had adapted her way of expressing herself to the scattered 'darlings' of ladies come for fittings. 'We must talk' was the euphemism for crisis, something difficult to be said. Zsuzsi has
decided upon a divorce. She's tried some other—what did she
say—solution, some way. But in the end. What. Well, they
both had been so young, back there . . . didn't know, really,
how either would be . . . If they hadn't had to leave—she
stopped. He waited. If we hadn't emigrated, maybe. He did
not interject but it was as if he had; Yes? If we had still been
there maybe we would have found ourselves going the same
way together. A change of tone, accusing herself: Maybe we
should have stayed. Who knows.

Maybe. The man she was with now, maybe it was the
owner of the house he saw, maybe the buyer or seller of another. She viewed—that's the word, clients are taken to view
what's on offer—walked through room after room, so many
prospective places for herself, the ballroom-size bedroom with
its vast draped bed, faintly giving the scent of perfume and

semen from an image of how it will be to make love there. The bathroom's sauna and the electric massage chair, ready to shudder. The kitchen with the face of the black cook placed among the shining equipment. Zsuzsana has found home.

He is in exile.

the second sense

The senses 'usually reckoned as five—sight, hearing, smell, taste, touch.'

—*Oxford English Dictionary*

SHE'S never felt any resentment that he became a musician and she didn't. Hardly call her amateur flute-playing a vocation. Envy? Only pride in the achievement he was born for. She sits at a computer in a city government office, earning under pleasant enough conditions a salary that at least has provided regularly for their basic needs while his remuneration for the privilege of being cellist in a symphony orchestra has been sometimes augmented by chamber music engagements, sometimes not; and in the summer, off-season for the orchestra, he was dependent on these performances on the side.

Their social life is in his professional circle, fellow musicians, music critics, aficionados whose connections ensure they have free tickets, and the musical families in which most of the orchestra members grew up, piano-teacher or choir-singing mothers and church-organist fathers. When people among them remember to give her the obligatory polite attention, with the question, What do you do?, and she tells them, it's clear that they wonder what she and the cellist who is married to her have in common. As for her, she found when still adolescent—the time for discoveries about parental limitations—that her cheerful father with his sports shop, beguiling heartiness a qualification for that business, and her mother with her groupies exchanging female reproductive maladies from conception to menopause, did not have in their comprehension what it was she Wanted To Do. A school outing had taken her to a concert where at sixteen she heard coming out of the slim tube held in human lips the call of the flute. Much later, she was able to identify the auditory memory as Mozart's Flute Concerto no. 2 in D, K. 314. Meanwhile, attribution didn't matter any more than the unknown name of a bird that sang heart-piercingly hidden in the parents' garden. The teacher who had arranged the cultural event was understanding enough to put the girl in touch with a youth musical group in the city; she baby-sat at weekends to pay for the hire of a flute and began to attempt to learn how to produce with her own breath and fingers something of what she had heard.

He was among The Youth Players. His instrument was the very antithesis of the flute. When they came to know one another part of the language of early attraction was a kind of repartee about this, show-off, slangy, childish. The sounds he drew from the overgrown violin between his knees: the complaining moo of a sick cow; the rasp of a blunt saw; a long fart. —Excuse me!— he would say, with a clownish lift of eyebrows and down-twisted mouth. The instrument was the cello, like her flute a second-hand donation to the Players from the estate of some old man or woman who left behind what was of no interest to family descendants. Alaric tended it in a sensuous way that if she had not been so young and innocent she could have read as an augur of how his love-making would begin.

Within a year his exceptional talent was recognised by the professional musicians who coached the young people voluntarily, and the cello was declared his, no longer on loan. They played together when alone, to amuse themselves and secretly imagine they were already in concert performance, the low, powerful cadence coming from the golden-brown body of the cello making by contrast her flute voice sound more that of a squeaking mouse than it would have, heard solo. In time, she reached a certain level of minor accomplishment. He couldn't lie to her. They had with the complicity of his friends found some place where they could make love—for her the first time—and out of a commitment to sincerity beyond their years, he couldn't deceive her and let her suffer the disillusions of persisting with a career not open to her level of performance. Already she had been hurt, dismayed at being replaced by other young flautists when ensembles were chosen for public performances by 'talented musicians of the future'.

You'll always have the pleasure of playing the instrument you love best. She would always remember what she said: The cello is the instrument I love best.

They grew up enough to leave whatever they had been told was home, the parents. They worked as waiters in a restaurant, he gave music lessons in schools, they found a bachelor pad in the rundown part of town where most whites were afraid to live because blacks had moved there since segregation was outlawed. In the generosity of their passionate happiness they had the expansive impossible need to share something of it, the intangible become tangible, bringing up to their kitchen nook a young man who played pennywhistle *kwela* at the street corner, to have a real meal with them, not handout small change to be tossed into his cap. The white caretaker of the building objected vociferously. You mad. You mad or what. Inviting blacks to rob and murder you. I can't have it in the building.

Paula went to computer courses and became proficient. If you're not an artist of some kind, or a doctor, a civil rights lawyer, what other skill makes you of use in a developing country? Chosen, loved by the one you love; what more meaningful than being necessary to him in a practical sense as well, with the ability to support his vocation whose achievements are yours by proxy. 'What do you do?' Can't you see? She makes fulfilment possible, for both of them.

Children. Married more than a year, they discussed this, the supposedly natural progression in love. Postponed until next time. Next time, they reached the fact: as his unusual gifts began to bring engagements for guest performance at music festivals abroad, and opportunities to play with prestigious—soon to be famous—orchestras, the fact clearly was that he could not be a father home for the bedtime story every night, or to be reliably expected to watch schoolboy weekend soccer games at the same time as he was a cellist soon to have his name on CD labels. If she could get leave from her increasingly responsible job—not too difficult on occasion—to accompany him, she would not be able to shelve that other responsibility, care of a baby. They made the choice of what they wanted: each other, within a single career. Let a mother and tea-time friends focus on the hazards of reproduction, contemplating their own navel cord. Let other men seek immortality in progeny; music has no limits of a life-span. An expert told them the hand-me-down cello was at least seventy or eighty years old and the better for it.

One month—when was it—she found she was pregnant;

kept getting ready to tell him but didn't. He was going on a
concert tour in another part of the country and when he came
back there was nothing to tell. The process was legal, fortunately, under the new laws of the country, conveniently available at a clinic named for Marie Stopes, past campaigner for
women's rights over their reproductive system. Better not to
have him—what? Even regretful, maybe, you know how men
no matter how rewarded with success, buoyant with the tide
of applause, still feel they must prove themselves potent.
(Where had she picked up that? Eavesdropping adolescent, on
tea-parties . . .)

She was so much part of the confraternity of orchestras. The
rivalry among the players, all drowned out by exaltation of the
music they created together. The gossip—as she was not one
of them, both the men and women would trust her with indiscretions they wouldn't risk with one another. And when he
had differences with a guest conductor from Bulgaria or Tokyo
or god knows where, their egos as complex as the pronunciation of their names, his exasperation found relief as he unbur-
dened himself, in bed, of the podium dramas and moved on to
the haven of love-making. If she were in a low mood—bungles
of an inefficient colleague at work, her father's 'heart condition' and her mother's long complaints over the telephone
about his breaking doctor's orders with his whisky-swilling
golfers—the cello would join them in the bedroom and he'd
play for her. Sometimes until she fell asleep to the low tender
tones of what had become his voice, to her, the voice of the big
curved instrument, its softly-buffed surface and graceful bulk
held close against his body, sharing this intimacy which was
hers. At concerts when his solo part came she did not know

she was smiling in recognition that here was the voice she would have recognised anywhere among other cellists bowing other instruments.

Each year, music critics granted, he played better. Exceeded himself. When distinguished musicians came for the symphony and opera season it was appropriate that he and she would entertain them at the house far from the pad they'd once dossed down in. Where others might keep a special piece of furniture, some inheritance, there stood in the livingroom, retired, the cello he'd learned to play on loan. He now owned an Amati, mid-18th-century cello found for him by a dealer in Prague. He had been hesitant. How could he spend such a fortune. But she was taken aback, indignant as if someone already had dared remark on presumptuous extravagance. An artist doesn't care for material possessions as such. You're not buying a Mercedes, a yacht! He had bought a voice of incomparable beauty, somehow human though of a subtlety and depth, moving from the sonority of an organ to the faintest stir of silences no human voice could produce. He admitted as if telling himself in confidence, as much as her, this instrument roused skilled responses in him he hadn't known.

In the company of guests whose life was music as was his, he was generous as a pop singer responding to fans. He would bring out the precious presence in its black reliquary, free it and settle himself to play among the buffet plates and replenished wine glasses. If he'd had a few too many he'd joke, taking her by the waist a moment, I'm just the *wunderkind* brought in to thump out *Für Elise* on the piano, and he'd play so purely, that the voice of the aristocratic cello she knew as well as she had that of the charity one, made all social exchange strangely trivial. But the musicians, entrepreneurs and guests favoured to be among them, applauded, descended upon him, the husbands and gays hunching his shoulders in their grasp, the women giving the accolade and sometimes landing on his lips. It wasn't unusual for one of the distinguished male guests—not the Japanese—specially the elderly German or Italian conductors, to make a pass at her. She knew she was attractive enough, intelligent enough musically and otherwise (even her buffet was good), for this to happen, but she was aware that it was really the bloom on her of being the outstandingly gifted cellist's woman which motivated these advances. Imagine if, next time the celebrated cellist played under your baton in Strasbourg, you would be able to remark aside to another musician your own age, 'And his wife's pretty good, too, in bed.' Once the guests had gone, host and hostess laughed in the bedroom about the attention paid flirtatiously he hadn't failed to notice. The cello stood grandly against the wall. Burglaries are common in the suburbs and there are knowledgeable gangs who don't look for TV sets and computers but for paintings and other valuable objects. If anyone broke in they'd have to come to the bedroom to catch sight of his noble Amati, and face the revolver kept under his pillow.

Bach, Mozart, Hindemith, Cage, Stockhausen, Glass are no longer regarded in the performance world patronisingly as music blacks neither enjoy nor understand, don't play. The national orchestra which was his base, while his prestige meant he could absent himself whenever he was invited to festivals or to join a string ensemble on tour, had a black trombonist and a young second violinist with Afro braids that fell about her ebony neck as she wielded her bow. She spoke German to a visiting Austrian conductor; she'd had a scholarship to study in Strasbourg. Professional musicians have always been a league of nations, for a time the orchestra had a tympanist from Brazil. He became a particular friend, taken into the house on occasion as a live-in guest, and to keep her company when the beautiful cello accompanied its player overseas.

She was aware that, without a particular ability of her own outside the everyday competence in commercial communications, she was privileged enough to have an interesting life: a remarkably talented man whose particular milieu was also hers.

What was the phrase—she 'saw the world', often travelling with him. She'd arranged leave, to accompany the string ensemble to Berlin, one of the many musical events in commemoration of Mozart's two-and-a-half-century birth date, but couldn't go after all because her father was dying—cheerfully, but her mother must be supported.

The ensemble met with exceptional success, where there were musicians of high reputation from many countries. He brought back a folder full of press cuttings—a few in English—glowing. He tipped his head dismissively; maybe you can become inured to praise, in time. Or he was tired, drained by the demands of his music. She had suggestions for relaxation—a film, a get-together dinner, away from concert-hall discipline, with the ensemble musicians, one becomes close to people, a special relationship she's long recognised in him, with whom something has been achieved in common. He was not enthusiastic. Next week, next week. He took the revered cello out of its solitude in the case carved to its shape and played, to himself. To her—well, she was in the room, those evenings.

It is his voice, that glorious voice of his cello; saying something different, not speaking to her but some other.

He makes love to her, isn't that always the signal of return when he's been away?

There's a deliberation in the caresses. She's almost moved to say stupidly what they'd never thought to say between them, do you still love me?

He begins to absent himself from her at unexplained times or for obligations that he must know she knows don't exist.

The voice of the cello doesn't lie.

How to apply to the life of this man the shabby ordinary circumstance, what's the phrase? He's having an affair. Artists of any kind attract women. They scent some mysterious energy of devotion there, that will always be the rival of their own usually reliable powers of seduction. Something that will be kept from even the most desired woman. Who'd know that attraction better than herself; but for her that other, mysterious energy of devotion, made of love a threesome. The cello with its curved body reverentially in the bedroom.

What woman.

At music festivals around the world the same orchestral players, the same chamber music quartets and trios keep meeting in different countries, they share a map of common experience, live in the same hotels, exchange discoveries of restaurants, complaints about concert-hall acoustics and enthusiasm over audience response. If it were to be some musician encountered on a particular tour, that didn't necessarily mean the affair was a brief one that ended when the man and woman each went their way seas and continents apart; they might meet again, plan to, at the next festival somewhere else in the world—Vienna, Jerusalem, Sydney, where he had played or was contracted to play soon. The stimulation not only of performance before an unknown audience but of meeting again, the excitement of being presented with the opportunity to take up something interrupted.

Or was the woman nearer home. A member of the national orchestra in which he and his cello were star performers. That was an identification she found hard to look for, considering their company of friends in this way. A young woman, of course, a younger woman than herself. But wasn't that just the inevitable decided at her mother's tea-table forum. The clarinet player was in her late Forties, endowed with fine breasts in décolleté and a delightful wit. There was often repartee between them, the clarinet and the cello, over drinks. The pianist, young with waist-length red-out-of-the-bottle hair, was a lesbian kept under strict guard by her woman. The third and last female musician among the orchestra components was also the last one would be crass enough to think of: she was Khomotso, the second violinist of extraordinary talent, one of the two black musicians. She was *so* young; she had given birth to an adored baby who for the first few months of life had been brought in the car of Khomotso's sister to rehearsals, so that the mother could suckle the infant there. The director of the orchestra gave an interview to a Sunday newspaper about this, as an example of the orchestra's transformation to the human values of the new South Africa. The violinist was certainly the prettiest, the most desirable of the women in whose company the cellist spent the intense part of his days and nights, but respect, *his* human feeling, would be stronger than sexual attraction, his identification with her as a musician making her way would taboo distracting her from that. As for him, wouldn't it look like the Old South Africa, white man 'taking advantage' of the precariously balanced life of a young black woman.

His lover might be one of faithful concert-season-goers who gave post-performance parties.

He had a lunchtime friendship with one of the male regulars, an industrialist, amateur viola player with a fine music library from which he was made free to borrow. So it might be one of the wives of such men. Many of these were themselves career women, much younger than the wealthy husbands, bringing intelligence of commitment to ideas and activities outside the arts, as well as what he might see as sexual availability.

It was no longer assumed she would be with him as she always had been when he accepted invitations to receptions or private houses; the unspoken implication was that these were now strictly professional. He never suggested what also had been assumed, that when he was to give a recital in another city within their home country, of course she would be there; he packed the overnight bag open on their bed, took up the black-clad body of the cello and kissed her goodbye. There were dutiful acts of well-spaced intercourse as if it were routine as regular intervals for a haircut. She began to want to avoid the approach in bed; and then grew fearful she would send him to the other woman by suggesting she did not desire him; and at the same time she terribly wanted to put her hands, her mouth on the body beside her, no matter the humiliation of what he followed like a medical procedure prescribed to satisfy her. A bill to be paid.

She waited for him to speak. About what had happened. To trust the long confidence between them. He never did. She did not ask because—she was also afraid that what happened once admitted, it would be irrevocably real. One night he got up in the dark, took the cello out of its bed and played. She woke to the voice, saying something passionately angry in its deepest bass. Then there came the time when—was it possible for this to be, in his magnificent, exquisite playing—there was a disharmony, the low notes dragging as if the cello refused him. Nights, weeks, the same.

So. She knew the affair was over. She felt a pull of sadness—for him. For herself, nothing. By never confronting him she had stunned herself.

Soon he came to her again. The three of them, he, she and the cello against the wall, were together.

He makes love better than ever before remembered, caresses not known, more subtle more anticipatory of what can be roused in her, what she's capable of feeling, needing. As if he's had the experience of a different instrument to learn from.

the third sense

The senses 'usually reckoned as five—sight, hearing, smell, taste, touch.'

—*Oxford English Dictionary*

HE's the owner of one of the private airlines who have taken up the internal routes between small cities and local areas the national airline, flying at astronomical heights to five continents, hasn't bothered with. Until lately, that is, when their aircraft with full-length sleeper beds and gourmet menus haven't succeeded in cosseting them against falling profits. Now they want to pick up cents on the local routes' discount market, enter into competition with modest craft flitting to unimportant places on home ground.

But that wouldn't have anything to do with this night.

Could have been some other night (Tuesdays he plays squash) if it didn't happen to be when there was a meeting of private airline owners to discuss their protest against the national carrier's intention as a violation of the law of unfair competition, since the great span of the national wings is sub-sidised by taxpayers' money. She didn't go along to listen in on the meeting because she was behind time with marking papers in media studies from her students in that university department. She was not alone at her desk, their dog lay under it at her feet, a fur-flounced English setter much loved by master and mistress, particularly since their son went off to boarding school. Dina the darling held the vacant place of only child. So intelligent, she even seemed to enjoy music; *The Pearl Fishers* CD was playing and she wasn't asleep. Well, one mustn't become a dotty dog lover, Dina was probably waiting to catch his footfall at the front door.

It came when the last paper was marked and being shuffled together with the rest, for tomorrow; she got up, stretching as she was instructed at aerobics class, and followed the dog's scramble downstairs.

He was securing the door with its locks and looped chain, safety for their night, and they exchanged, How'd it go, any progress, Oh round in circles again, that bloody lawyer didn't show—but the master didn't have to push down the dog's usual bounding interference when the master came home from anywhere, anytime. *Hullo my girl*—his expected greeting ignored, no paws landing in response on his shoulders. While he was questioned about the evening and they considered coffee or a drink before bed, you choose, the dog was intently scenting round his shoes. He must have stepped in something. As they went upstairs together, he turning from above her to repeat exasperated remarks about why he was so late, how long the meeting dragged on, the dog pushed past her to impede him, dilated nose rising against his pants' legs. Dina, down! What d'you think you're doing! He slapped the furry rump to make her mount ahead. She stood at the top of the stairs in the hunting dog's point stance, faced at him. Dina'd never been in the field, he was not a hunting man. Some displaced atavistic tic come up in an indulged housepet.

· While they undressed they decided for coffee. Dina didn't jump on their bed in customary invitation for them to join her, she was giving concentrated attention to his discarded pants, shirt, shoes. Must be the shoes that perfumed his attraction. Doggy-doo, Eva said, Wait a minute, don't put them on the rug, I'll run the tap over the soles: Michael laughed at the crumple of distaste lifting her nose, her concern for the kelim. In the bathroom, instead, she wet a streamer of the toilet roll, rubbed each sole and flushed the paper down the bowl: although there was no mess clinging to the leather a smell might remain. She propped his shoes to dry, uppers resting against the wall of the shower booth.

When she came back into the bedroom he'd dropped off, asleep, lying in his pyjama pants, the newspaper untidy across his naked chest: opened his eyes with a start.

Still want coffee?

He yawned assent.

Come, Dina. Bedtime.

As a child enjoys a cuddle in the parents' bed before banishment to his own, it was the dog's routine acceptance that she would descend to her basket in the kitchen when the indulgence was declared over. Tonight she wasn't on the bed with master, she got up slowly from where she lay beside a chair, turned her head in some quick last summons to sniff at his clothes lying there, and went down to her place while Eva brewed the coffee.

They drank it side by side in bed. I didn't make it too strong? Looks as if nothing could keep you awake tonight, anyway.

There were disturbed nights, these days, when she would be awakened by the sleepless changed rhythm of the breathing beside her, the interrupted beat of the heart of intimacy shared by lovers over their sixteen years. He had put all their funds into his airline. Flight Hadeda (her choice of the name of ibis that flew over the house calling out commandingly). Profits of the real estate business he'd sold; her inheritance from her father's platinum mining interests. Those enterprises of old regime white capitalism were not the way to safe success in a mixed economy—politically correct capitalism. Such enterprises were now anxiously negotiating round affirmative action requirements that this percentage or that of holdings in their companies be reserved for black entrepreneurs with workers becoming token shareholders in stock exchange profits. A small airline, dedicated to solving something of the transport problems of a vast developing country, had patriotic significance. If Michael and his partner are white, the cabin attendants, one of the pilots and an engineer are black. Isn't it an honest not exploitative initiative on which they've risked everything? She knows what keeps him open-eyed, dead-still in the night: if the national airline takes up the homely routes its resources will ground the Everything in loss. Once or twice she has broken the rigid silence intended to spare her; the threat is hers, as well. There is no use to talk about it in the stare of night; she senses that he takes her voice's entry to his thoughts maybe as some sort of reproach: the airline is his venture, way-out, in middle age.

The coffee cups are on the floor, either side of their bed. She turned on her elbow to kiss him goodnight but he lifted a hand and got up to put on the pyjama jacket. She liked his bare chest near her, the muscles a little thicker—not fat—than they used to be; when you are very tired you feel chilly at night. Climbing back to bed he stretched to close the light above. His sigh of weariness was almost a groan, let him sleep, she did not expect him to turn to her. Let the mutual heart beat quietly. Before moving away for private space they mostly fell asleep in what she called the spoon-and-fork way: she on her side and his body folded along her back, or him on his other side and she curved along his. Of course he was the spoon when enveloping her back in protection from shoulders to thighs, her body was the slighter line of the fork, its light bent tines touching the base of his nape, her breasts nestled under his dorsal muscles. This depended haphazardly on who turned this or that side first, tonight he rolled onto his right, approaching deep sleep giving him a push that way. The gentle impetus reached her to follow, round against him. The softness of breasts in opposition to the male rib cage and spine are one of the wordless questions and answers between men and women. In offended vanity which long survives, she never forgot that once, in early days, he'd remarked as an objective observation, she didn't have really good legs; her breasts were his admiring, lasting discovery. In bantering moods of passion she'd tell him he was a tit man and he would counter with mock regret he hadn't ever had a woman with those ample poster ones on display. In tonight's version of the spoon-and-fork embrace she always had her closed eyes touched against his hair and her nose and lips in the nape of his neck. She liked to breathe there, into him and breathe him in, taking possession he was not conscious of and was yet the essence of them both. These were not the sort of night moments you tell the other, anyway they half-belong to the coming state of sleep, the heightened awareness of things that's called the unconscious. None of his business, secret even from herself that she enters him there as, female, she can't the way he enters her. Or it's just something else; the way you would bury your face in that incredibly innocent sensuous touch and smell of an infant's hollow under the back of its skull. But that's not a memory which persists from the distant infancy of a fifteen-year-old whose voice has broken. She moves her face, herself, into the nape as she does without at first meeting the skin, not to disturb, the touch of the lips to come after the gentlest touch of her breathing there—

She's sniffing. She's drawing back a little from the hollow smooth and unlined as if it were that of a man of twenty. Comes close again. Scenting. Her nose drawn tight, then nostrils flared to short intakes of whatever. Scenting. She knows their smell, the smell of his skin mingled with what she is, a blend of infusions from the mysterious chemistry of different activities in different parts of their bodies, giving off a flora of flesh juices, the intensity or delicacy of sweat, semen, cosmetics, saliva, salt tears: all become an odour distilled as theirs alone.

Scenting on him the smell of another woman.

She moved carefully out of bed. He was beyond stirring as her warmth left him. She went into the bathroom. Switched on the light above the mirror and forced herself to look at herself. To make sure. It was facing a kind of photography no-one had invented. It wasn't the old confrontation with oneself. There was another woman who occupied the place of that image. Smell her.

She, herself, was half-way down the passage darkness to the bed in the room that served as guest and storeroom when— despising that useless gesture, she went back. In their bed she lay spaced away from where she would allow herself to approach, scenting again what she already had. Rationality attacked: why didn't he shower instead of dozing bare-chested and then climbing into bed. Yes, he'd got up and put on the pyjama jacket; in place of the shower's precaution. He showered when he came home after squash games. Was it really from the squash courts he returned, always, Tuesday nights.

It wasn't that she didn't allow herself to think further; she could not think. A blank. So that it might not begin to fill, she left their bed again as carefully, silently as the first time, and in the bathroom found his bottle of sleeping pills (she never took soporifics, a university lectureship and the take-off and landing of a risky airline enterprise did not share the same 'stress'). She shook out what looked like a plastic globule of golden oil and swallowed it with gulps of tap water cupped in her hand. When she woke from its unfamiliar stun in the morning he was coming from the bathroom shiningly freshly shaved, called, Hullo darling; as he did 'Hullo my girl' in affectionate homecoming, to their dog.

EVA and Michael Tate lived the pattern of the working week, seven days and the next seven days differentiated only by the disruptions of Michael's alternations of tentative hopes and anxiety about negotiations with the national airline that might bring not a solution for Flight Hadeda's survival but a bankruptcy as its resolution. 'That's no exaggeration.' He rejected her suggestion that as negotiations were lagging on, this was surely a good sign that the government was at last having doubts. After all their rapping of the private sector over the knuckles for not taking enough responsibility in new ways to develop the infrastructure . . . Beginning to listen to the private airlines. 'Government could have just gone ahead and granted licences to the national after that window-dressing democratic first meeting with all of you. Why didn't it? I think it's tip-toeing round a compromise.'

He had pulled his upper and lower lips in over his teeth as if to stop what he didn't want to say.

There were also words she didn't want to say.

She did something out of her anger and disbelief, that disgusted her. But she did it. She called the squash club on a Tuesday night and asked to speak to Michael Tate. The receptionist told her to hold: for her, an admonition not to breathe. The voice came back, Sorry, Mr Tate is not here tonight. 'Sorry' the regret a form of colloquial courtesy personnel are taught.

Eva read in bed and the dog's indulgence, there with her, was extended. Music accompanied them and she did not look at her watch until the dog jumped off and made for the stairs. Michael was back. And early. Down, Dina, down! They were in the bedroom doorway, the dog with paws leapt to his shoulders. Dina's come to accept what she scents as part of the aura, now, of the couple and the house, she does not have to recall the atavism of hunting instincts.

Eva does not remark on the hour. And he doesn't remark that he finds her already gone to bed. Perhaps he isn't aware of her. She's never experienced coming home to one man from another, although she once had a woman friend who said she managed it with some sort of novel pleasure.

'Win or lose?' Eva asked. The old formula response would be in the same light exchange; a mock excuse if he'd been out of form, mock boast if he'd played well—they knew Tuesdays were for keeping fit rather than sport; avoiding the onset of that male pregnancy, a middle-age belly.

'I think I'm getting bored with the club. All my contemporaries working out. Most of us past it.'

She tried to keep to the safe formula. 'So you lost for once!'

He did not answer.

He'd gone to the bathroom; there was the rainfall susurrus—he was taking a shower this time. When he came back she saw him naked; yes, nothing unusual about that, the chest she liked, the stomach with the little fold—no, it's muscle, no, no, not fat—the penis in its sheath of foreskin. But she saw the naked body as she had seen herself in the bathroom mirror that first night when she and the dog scented him.

He spoke, turned from her, getting into pyjamas. 'It looks worse every day. There's a leak that's come to us. Adams knows one of their officials. They've had approved a schedule of the routes they intend to take up. Analysing cost structures if bookings are to be taken only online, cut out the travel agents' levy on passengers.'

'But you can do the same.'

'We can? Travel agents feed us passengers as part of overseas visitors' round-trip tours. We can't afford to ditch them.' He came to the bed.

'Aren't you taking Dina?'

Recalled to where he was from wherever he had been, he put his hand on the dog's head and the two went to the stairs. When he reappeared he got into bed and did not lean for the good-night kiss. The alternate to his reason for avoidance could be the despairing abstraction: distrait. As Michael turned out their light he spoke aloud but not to her. 'Hadeda's down. Scrap.'

For the first time in sixteen years there was no possibility of one comforting the other in embrace. She said in the dark 'You

can't give up.' She didn't know whether this was a statement
about Flight Hadeda or a bitter conclusion about where he had
been, this and other nights.

They did continue what the new millennium vocabulary
terms 'having sex' not making love, from time to time, less often than before. This would be when they had had a night out
with friends, drinking a lot of wine, or had stood around at her
duty academic celebrations when everyone drank successive
vodkas, gins or whiskys to disprove the decorum of academia.

So, it was possible for him to desire her then. Hard to
understand. She's always refused to believe the meek sexist
acceptance that men's desire is different from women's. When
they went through the repertoire of caresses real desire was not
present in her body; for her, as it must be for him, desire must
belong with another woman.

She was looking for the right moment to come out with it.
How to say what there was to be said. The 'Are you having an
affair' of soap operas. 'You are having an affair'; restating the
obvious. 'You're making love to some woman, even the dog
smells her on you.' Away with euphemisms. When to speak?
At night? Early in the morning, a breakfast subject? Before
Patrick came home for the holidays? What happens when such
things are said. Would they both go to work after the breakfast, take their son to the movies, act as if the words hadn't
been said, until he was out of the way back at school.

The night before Easter she was taking from the freezer a
lamb stew that was to be the last meal together before it was
spoken. What she would find the right way to say. When he
came home he closed the livingroom door behind him against
the entry of the dog and strode over to turn mute the voice of
the newscaster on the television.

'I'm shutting up shop. Just a matter of selling the two jets, no-one's going to be stupid enough to buy the licence. Fat hope of that. Adams and I have gone through the figures for the past eighteen months and even if the national thing weren't about to wipe us off it's there—we're flying steadily into loss.'

The brightly miming faces were exchanged on the screen while he said what he had to say.

'But we knew you'd have to rely on our capital for a least two years before you'd get into profit, it's not the same issue as the national one.'

'The competition will make the other irrelevant, that's all. Why wait for that. Sell the planes. Won't make up the loss. The overdraft.'

'It'll be something.'

There were images dwelling on the dead lying somewhere, Afghanistan, Darfur, Iraq.

'For what. To do what.'

He's been a man of ideas, in maturity, with connections, friends in enterprises.

'You'll look around.' That's what he did before, set out to change his life from earthbound real estate to freedom of the sky.

He lifted his spread hands, palm up and let them drop as if they would fall from his wrists while the screen was filled by the giant grin-grimace of a triumphant footballer. 'How are we going to live in the meantime.'

'I don't bring in bread on the corporate scale, oh yes, but there's a good chance I'll be appointed head of the Department with the beginning of the new academic year.'

'It'll just about pay the fees at Patrick's millionaire school.' That school also, had been the father's ambitious mould-breaking choice for their son; if it was now a matter of reproach, the reproach was for himself, not a sharp reception of her provision of an interim rescue. Despair ravaged his face like the signs of a terminal illness.

She did not say what she had decided was the right time and the right words to say.

She saw he managed to eat a little of the lamb as some sort of acknowledgement of her offer.

EVA recalled that time, the Tuesday when he came home from the woman and said about his fellows at the squash court where he hadn't played with them—Sorry, Mr Tate is not here tonight—he was getting bored with the club, 'All my contemporaries working out. Most of us past it.'

Past it.

Too late. In middle age the schoolboy adventure of Flight Hadeda, even that night in unadmitted faltering, and threatened by the national carrier he had no means to counter. Inside Eva, sometimes softening; the failure accepted, perhaps he had been too tired, stressed's the cover-all word, to make love.

What other way to reassure, restore himself. Not past it; proof of the engendered male power of life, arousal to potency: by another woman.

Eva never confronted Michael with the smell of the woman scented on him. She did not know whether he saw the woman some other time, now that he had given up the Tuesday night squash club; when or whether he had given up the affair. She did not know, nor return by the means she and the dog possessed, for evidence.

ACKNOWLEDGEMENTS

Grateful acknowledgement is made to the following publications, in whose pages these stories first appeared:

Daedalus: "Tape Measure." *Granta*: "Beethoven Was One-Sixteenth Black." *The Guardian*: "Gregor" and "A Frivolous Woman." *Harper's Magazine*: "History." *New Statesman*: "Dreaming of the Dead" and "Mother Tongue." *The New Yorker*: "Alternative Endings: The Second Sense," "A Beneficiary," and "Safety Procedures." *Playboy*: "Alternative Endings: The Third Sense." *Salmagundi*: "Allesverloren." *Virginia Quarterly Review*: "Alternative Endings: The First Sense."

A NOTE ON THE AUTHOR

Nadine Gordimer's many novels include *The Lying Days* (her first novel), *The Conservationist*, joint winner of the Booker Prize, *Get A Life*, *Burger's Daughter*, *July's People*, *My Son's Story*, *None to Accompany Me*, *The House Gun* and *The Pickup*. Her collections of short stories include *Something Out There*, *Jump* and, most recently, *Loot*. She also edited the anthology of stories *Telling Tales*. In 1991 she was awarded the Nobel Prize for Literature, and in 2007 she received the Legion of Honour, France's highest accolade. She lives in South Africa.

A NOTE ON THE TYPE

The text of this book is set in Garamond 3. It is one of several versions of Garamond based on the designs of Claude Garamond. It is thought that Garamond based his font on Bembo, cut in 1495 by Francesco Griffo in collaboration with the Italian printer Aldus Manutius. Garamond types were first used in books printed in Paris around 1532. Many of the present-day versions of this type are based on the *Typi Academiae* of Jean Jannon cut in Sedan in 1615.

Claude Garamond was born in Paris in 1480. He learned how to cut type from his father and by the age of fifteen he was able to fashion steel punches the size of a pica with great precision. At the age of sixty he was commissioned by King Francis I to design a Greek alphabet, for this he was given the honourable title of royal type founder. He died in 1561.